PARADISE ICON
ANTHOLOGY 2023

Paradise ICON Copyright © 2023

This is a work of fiction. Names, characters, places, and incidents either are the product of the author's imagination or are used fictitiously. Any resemblance to actual persons, living or dead, events, or locales is entirely coincidental.

The following content is copyright 2023 by its respective authors:

"The Transfer of Venus" by Doug Engstrom
"The Chimera's Quiet Revolt" by Athena Foster
"Edgar's Foxes" by George Galuschak
"The Devil's Hand" by Jenna Hanchey
"Apartment 2B" by Ransom Noble
"House of the Gremlin" by Shannon Ryan
"Lussinaten" by Cath Schaff-Stump
"Raise Hell" by Miranda Suri
"The Grasshopper and the Dawn" by Stephanie Vance

All rights reserved. No part of this book may be reproduced or used in any manner without written permission of the copyright owner except for the use of brief quotations in critical articles, reviews, social media, and certain other noncommercial use permitted by copyright law. For more, address queries to editor Ransom Noble: noble.ransom@gmail.com.

Paradise Icon Anthology 2023

Douglas Engstrom
Athena Foster
George Galuschak
Jenna Hanchey
Ransom Noble
Shannon Ryan
Cath Schaff-Stump
Miranda Suri
Stephanie Vance

Edited by Ransom Noble

For Chris Cornell and Mom

Contents

Introduction	1
Devil's Hand *Jenna Hanchey*	3
The Grasshopper and the Dawn *Stephanie Vance*	13
The Transfer of Venus *Doug Engstrom*	35
Edgar's Foxes *George Galuschak*	45
Apartment 2B *Ransom Noble*	51
Lussinaten *Catherine Schaff-Stump*	59
The Chimera's Quiet Revolt *Athena Foster*	75
Raise Hell *Miranda Suri*	91
House of the Gremlin *Shannon Ryan*	105
Acknowledgements	133

Introduction

Perhaps it is fitting that I am editing and publishing the 2023 version of the Paradise ICON anthology because I first attended this group in 2013. I was intimidated by the other writers, and I was sure I didn't belong, but I made friends anyway, and I stayed.

This third anthology will help support ICON, Iowa's oldest science fiction convention, just like its predecessors. Paradise ICON attendees enjoy the home we have with ICON, and we create anthologies with the hope of it continuing indefinitely.

Here's a secret – I never knew I wrote horror until I came to ICON. It's not every story, but I do put some horror elements into some of my work. I'm not sure why I didn't see it before, but this group helped me to grow into a more confident writer and an author who is excited to make my own path into publishing.

Cath Schaff-Stump is our fearless leader, and I am very glad to have her at the helm. This book is dedicated to Chris Cornell, our too-soon gone friend, and also my mother who died last year. Many of the other writers within this group have become great friends over the years, and I look forward to seeing them every year. Also every year, I bring something to workshop so both my writing and my critiquing skills have grown.

I hope you enjoy this book as much as I loved putting it together. Each story – this year some were prompted by things we said in workshop and some were not – is in a little bit different niche in the speculative fiction umbrella. A couple of the prompts used this year: "Oh, it's the rain." "Your Gremlin energy is strong." "But what in Christianity makes sense?" "Revolution is so hard though."

I'm still waiting for the story that came from "I hope he gets dismembered soon." Maybe in a future anthology. I might even get to write it!

The Devil's Hand

Jenna Hanchey

The Devil glared over the top of his sunglasses as the demon chained to a rack in front of him screamed. "Right. What's this about again?"

"Well," Malphas squirmed, standing to his boss's left and holding his hell-issued clipboard unsteadily, "It's a little complicated."

"Explain it. I don't like to be kept waiting." The demon in front of them yelped, twisting to avoid a flaming rope bearing down on him.

Malphas took an unconscious step back, smoothing his suit and making sure nothing unsavory had landed on it. "Basically, Beelzebub here tried to, uh, well, expand the Domination Plan Subset C.4: Soul-Selling Initiative. But it, uh, did not go as planned."

The Devil gave Malphas a curious look. "'Soul-Selling Initiative?' Is that what you call that thing I do when I'm bored every hundred years or so, hanging out at the crossroads, getting motorcycle riders and fiddle players to make a bum deal?" The Devil pulled off his sunglasses in exasperation. "Look, I know you're convinced this corporate lingo is useful, but it's so unnecessarily complicated."

Malphas assiduously checked his notes. It also offered him a means of avoiding the point for another few seconds. "Yes, that's the Initiative alright." He paused. "And if you think the corporate lingo is unnecessarily complicated, you're really not going to like this next part."

"Why? What did he do that landed him *here*?" The Devil waved his arm, encompassing the formidable array of torturous paraphernalia arranged around poor Beelzebub.

Malphas gulped.

The Devil's next growl couldn't be ignored. "What did he do, Malphas?"

"He attempted to, well, *franchise* it, I guess you could say."

"Again, Malphas, with the lingo. Franchise?"

"Yes, sir. I mean, he was very committed, *very* committed to your instruction that the Devil's hand should be in everything. So he tried to find ways to get us into the tech world—you know, update our methods a bit." Malphas swallowed hard, knowing what often happened to messengers. "It's a great concept, in theory! He just took language directly from your eternally-binding contract that the humans sign their names to in order to sell their souls, and made sure it was a legally-binding part of all social media terms of service agreements."

The Devil was beginning to get frustrated, and that was never good. "That sounds great! Fools sign those all the time without reading them. So what? It didn't work?"

"Oh no, sir. The problem is that it *did*. Just not in the way he intended. Rather than, uh, selling souls to *us*, he may have written it such that each retweet or like or comment sells a piece of someone's soul to, well…to another human, sir."

The Devil whipped around to face Malphas, grabbing his broad red shoulders with both hands. "WHAT?"

Malphas remained remarkably composed, considering. "Yes," he squeaked, "Thus, all this." He waved his arm in feeble mimicry of his Master, though it couldn't move very far given the vice-like grip the Devil had on him.

Coughing lightly, the Lord of Smoke and Fire, Second-in-Command of All Hells, barely managed to force himself to say, "And there's more."

"How could there possibly be MORE?" The Devil roared.

"Although you have a formidable number of souls under your control in each of the Seven Hells, there population of the Earth has really expanded over the last century, exponentially, you know, and so you, uh, well, you seem to have lost the top position in terms of souls actually *owned*." Unable to stand his Master's stony silence, Malphas continued quickly, "You're no longer the official King of Hells, I'm sorry to say, because one human has managed to accumulate so many parts of souls that she technically has jurisdiction over your Lordship."

"SHE?" The Devil shook Malphas so hard that one of his wings broke under the force. "Are you telling me that the King of All Hells is now Taylor Swift or Beyoncé or some other vapid celebrity?!"

"Well, not exactly. Interestingly enough, the soul-selling calculations are not merely about *quantity* of followers or responses, but more substantially about the amount and quality of *emotional* investment made in the account being followed." In his enthusiasm for fascinating data, Malphas almost forgot he stood on quite treacherous ground. "Would you like to see the charts, I have them right here—"

"AAARRRGHH," the Devil growled, hurling Malphas into a glass-encrusted wall. "Tell me who *she* is."

Gritting his teeth, Malphas spoke through the pain. "Maude Mayberry, owner of Molasses, the Amazing Baking Cat."

§

Maude was having herself a delightful Tuesday before the Devil came a-knockin' at her door. She'd gotten just the most marvelous video of Molasses daintily tipping vanilla into her chess pie in the making, and an adorable reaction shot when the kitty licked some of the vile-tasting stuff from his paw. The chess pie was still in the oven, but Maude knew it'd turn out all perfect. Her baking always did.

"Chess pie's cooking up right now, folks. Betcha can't wait to see what it looks like!" Maude winked at the phone camera, wedged securely in the ringlight in front of her, as she slowly removed her apron. "And for all y'all out there stuck in the middle of something, worried about where life's going, feeling boxed in on all sides—oh, don't you worry, darlings! You're just like my lovely chess pie, here.

Don't worry your pretty little heads—sometimes you just need a little more baking time before you're ready for the next adventure."

"Meow!" Her midnight diva of a cat didn't like to be left out. Molasses leapt up onto the counter, and rolled in her discarded apron, wrapping himself up and batting the ties into the air. After a few seconds, he looked up at Maude, and she started their wrap-up, "That's all from Maude and Molasses for today, folks. We'll have a picture of that pie up here now as soon as it's done, for y'all to enjoy. And you know I'd love to see your lovely delicacies as well, so don't be shy in sharing!"

Placing her hand reverently on her chest, Maude signed off. "May your hearts grow enough to love all who's around you! I know mine has."

She'd just finished editing and posting the video when a thunderous knock shook the house to its very foundation. Shuffling in her cornflower slippers, Maude made her way through the living room, passing the white-painted shelves dripping with knick-knacks, and turned into the mud room to find Molasses hissing at the front door, back arched high as she'd ever seen.

"Hush, dearie," she scolded her companion lightly. "Just because they're rude doesn't mean we have to be." Molasses spat, but did as he was told. Maude nodded knowingly, and the sleek beast deftly hopped onto a nearby bench before pivoting to land square upon her right shoulder. Thus bastioned, Maude opened the door.

Two men stood there, one carrying a briefcase and the other looking like smoke was about to come out of his ears. The fuming one had clearly been doing the knocking, fist still raised in the air. Their dark hair curled around pale faces like snakes in the shadows.

"Can I help you?" Maude asked politely.

"Yes ma'am," answered the fidgety one with the briefcase. "I hope so. You see, we have a, um, financial proposition for you."

"For me?" The old woman narrowed her eyes, evaluating the strange pair.

"A very lucrative proposition, I think you'll find. One that a wise woman like yourself is sure to find appealing." The fuming one shifted quickly from fiery rage to charming smolder. Molasses' claws dug into her shoulder, and Maude pursed her lips. She'd never had time for men that thought they could get on with secretive smiles and pretty words. And certainly not ones who tried to tell her what to think. Besides that, Molasses could spy a scoundrel a mile away.

"Well, I sure do appreciate y'all coming by, but I've got a pie in the oven and a little darling here to feed." Maude started to close the door, but a sharply polished black shoe wedged in before she could.

"We will be coming in." Flames rose in the smolderer's eyes.

"Well now, I don't think so," replied Maude, unafraid but getting angry herself. No one came into her house without her say so. "Take a seat there on the porch. I'll bring out some lemonade, and then I'll let y'all say your piece."

She locked the door behind her as she went to fetch the lemonade. No reason to take chances with folks like these. Molasses meowed quizzically, still riding atop her slightly stooped shoulder.

"Don't worry, darling. I've got this under control."

§

Malphas winced at the squeak in his rocking chair. He did not like the way this was going, not one bit. The Devil refused to sit, pacing back and forth across the porch, as they waited for the tottering hag to return. Which felt like it was taking forever. Every second they spent here meant more souls lost...which for Malphas, meant more possibility of taking Beezlebub's place on the rack when they returned.

He pulled out the paperwork and set it on his lap, absent-mindedly pushing the edges to make sure everything aligned. Though it would be best for her to sign in blood, always preferred, he guessed they weren't about to get that woman to so much as prick her little finger. Instead, he settled for a fancy fountain pen, which he carefully laid atop the perfectly-stacked pile.

He was almost beginning to enjoy the back-and-forth motion of his strange seat when the door creaked open and Maude trundled out. In spite of himself, Malphas was quite impressed at the old woman's ability to balance a tray carrying a pitcher of lemonade, three glasses, three plates and accompanying forks, and a steaming chess pie, all while a growling cat sat perched on her shoulder. The Devil stopped his pacing, whirling around to watch as Maude carefully set the tray down and started slicing the dessert.

"Well, alright now, gentlemen," Maude finally allowed after everyone had been served. "What's this all about?"

The Devil's gaze fell on him hard, like the asteroid they sent to eliminate the pesky dinosaurs. Between that and Maude's stony expression, Malphas was quite uncomfortable. "So, um," he sputtered, fibbing poorly, "we represent a conglomeration of media companies whose platforms you use. We need you to sign an updated Terms of Service agreement in order to continue utilizing our products. We've brought the paperwork over ourselves so as not to interrupt your usage. We are willing to offer a generous payment to ensure the timeliness of your cooperation."

"I'm just an old lady making baking and cat videos. I may not be a 'techno indigenous,' or whatever they call the young folk, but I know my way around. So I don't see why you two ill-dressed ruffians have come knocking on my door, rather than making me click something online before signing in again."

Malphas squirmed in his chair. "Well…"

The Devil interrupted before he could come up with a satisfactory answer. "You see, ma'am," his Lordship said with a smarmy grin, "we try to *personally* support those who are doing excellent work, such as yourself, with your—" he paused, visibly composing himself, "—cat videos. You might think of this as a bonus. One quite deserved for all your viral posts! And, while we're here," he shrugged, arms open wide, "we thought we may as well just kill two humans with one axe and update your Terms of Service at the same time."

Malphas grimaced at the wording, shooting a worried glance at the woman across from him. His Lordships' phrasing was not always up to human standards.

Maude rocked thoughtfully in her chair, no reaction visible in her comportment. The Devil was standing, but stationary at least. The lemonade seemed to have calmed his agitation. The two demons waited, one fearful and the other impatient, to hear what Maude would say.

Molasses purred loudly from the old woman's lap, the only sound infiltrating the tense silence.

"It seems like I've got you two over a barrel, now, don't it?" Maude finally replied.

Although the Second in Command of All Hells had heard the phase about one's heart dropping into one's stomach before, this was the first time he had ever felt it.

"What?" The Devil's body tightened, all attempts at charm gone.

"I ain't gonna sign your papers, and I don't s'pose y'all can do anything about it."

"*Woman*, you have *no idea* who you are dealing with!" The Devil shouted, advancing on Maude from over Malphas' shoulder.

"Mmmm, I think you got that backwards, now," Maude said tightly, her words as cold as the Devil's were hot. "You don't know me at all."

The Devil froze, thrown off by the edge to Maude's tone. Malphas surprised himself by having to fight back a grin. No one had ever spoken to the King of All Hells like that! He took a bite of pie in his delight, but almost choked as realization landed. He looked at Maude, eyes wide. His Lordship was not, actually, the King of All Hells anymore. Malphas bolted upright, throwing his rocking chair off balance and sending the pie flying into his pristine suit.

Maude stroked her cat, a small smirk on her face. "Y'all can go on back to the Devil now and tell him I'm not signing any new terms. I read every little thing I'm asked to put my name to, twice if need be to understand it. I know the power of names, you see. And mine means something. I don't give it out lightly.

"So, I also know about them souls I've gone and collected. And seeing as I ain't in this for the money, y'all got nothing left to offer me."

This time the demon couldn't hold back. An unfortunate giggle erupted from Malphas's chest, at the very moment that the Devil exploded from his suit—both cloth and skin—to appear in his full, terrifying glory right there on Maude Mayberry's porch. Malphas clapped a hand over his treacherous mouth.

"How *dare* you fail to recognize me! You think me a mere *minion*? Equal to *this* pathetic creature?!" Malphas' eyes flared as the Devil gestured at him dismissively. "Look upon me! I am the Lord of Lies, Fallen Star of the High Heavens, Exalted King of the Seven Hells! You shall bow before me, hag!" The horned crimson beast thundered at Maude, unfurling his bat-like wings and lifting clenched fists high into the air.

But Maude just kept rocking and smiling and petting her cat.

Before he knew what he was doing, Malphas heard himself say, "Well, actually, I believe *Maude* here is officially the Exalted King of the Seven Hells, at the moment."

Maude grinned at him, and winked. "And from what I gather," she continued, "That's the only one of your titles that holds water, the rest being nicknames and such. I told you," she said calmly, rocking back and forth, "I know the power of names."

The Devil raged and roared, but the sound faded to white noise as Malphas held the keen old woman's gaze. He felt himself begin to relax for the first time in…well, an eternity. Picking a glob of buttery goodness off his chest, he leaned back and popped it into his mouth, savoring the sweet taste as it spread across his tongue, before chasing it with a dash of cool lemonade.

§

Maude placed her hands on her hips as she surveyed her new territory. "We got a lot o' work to do here, Malphas my boy."

As an eternal being, Malphas was fairly certain he had never been referred to as a "boy" before, but coming from the Exalted Maude, he didn't mind. She clapped a hand on his shoulder. "And I'm going be trusting you to help me get all these other folks on board."

Malphas nodded, looking over his notes. "Right, I think I've got the design changes down. I'll put a few hundred demons on it, and we'll have the groundwork set for the new Seven Levels of Community in no time." Pausing, he leaned down to pet Molasses, who was vibrating as he wound around the demon's hooved feet. Looking up again, he bit his lip. "I'm afraid I just don't quite understand the *logic* of it, however."

"Well, son, it's like this: I may have collected bits and pieces of a whole heap of souls, enough to make me High King of the Seven Communities, Ruler of the New Hell, but you see they have also been collecting pieces of mine all that time, too. Every follower what made me smile, or I happened to like their photo of my recipe—they got a piece of me with that like, just like I got a piece of them. So I'm thinking the New Hell has got to be a reflection of the fact that we *all* own pieces of souls, see? I'm figuring we teach everybody to value the souls they've got, and remember that other folks out there are cherishing their soul, too."

She laughed heartily. "As far as I can figure, this whole thing started when the Devil wanted his hand in everything and everyone. Well, now, I suppose we've done it! 'Cept I'M the Devil now, and I may have my hand in everyone, but they've got theirs in me too!"

"And, uh," Malphas jotted something down, "so that means part of the ways Community placement is decided is by intensity of soul-attachments between the different, uh, folks?" He stumbled over the last word. Residents of Hell had traditionally had much more colorful appellations.

"See, you get it!" Maude looked at him proudly. "You learn quickly, Malphas. I'm right pleased to have you as my Second in Command."

Molasses leapt up onto a dark spire of rock, which reminded the demon that the fortifications definitely needed a new color scheme. The fretting feline mewed at Maude, twirling his tail in slight distress.

"Aw now, don't you worry, darling," Maude answered. "I know where that Devil's gone. I ain't the new Lord of Hell for nothing. Let him try to meet with those technological overlords for as long as he wants. They can talk until they're blue in the face, but they can't stop us now."

Leaning over slightly, the Ruler of New Hell, Designer of Community Living, gestured for Molasses to take his familiar post on her shoulder. "Let's go and look at the progress in Community Three to take your little mind off things." She smirked, and the demon at her side could have sworn he saw an ocean wave crash in her eyes. "I'm tellin' you again, I got this under control."

Watching Maude slowly shuffle away, Malphas felt an unusual pressure in his broad, red torso. He began to intuit the meaning of another human turn of phrase as his chest expanded, releasing his heart to take flight. Perhaps, thought The Lord of Sugar and Water, Second-in-Command of the Seven Levels of Community, this was hope.

Jenna Hanchey has been called a "badass fairy" and she attempts to live up to the title. A professor of critical/cultural studies at Arizona State University, her research looks at how speculative fiction can imagine decolonization and bring it into being. Her own writing tries to support this project of creating better futures for us all. Her stories have appeared in *Nature, Daily Science Fiction, Little Blue Marble,* and *If There's Anyone Left,* among other venues. She's Poetry Editor at *Orion's Belt,* and a member of the Codex Writers Forum. Follow her adventures at www.jennahanchey.com.

THE GRASSHOPPER AND THE DAWN

STEPHANIE VANCE

What if my youth were white with age's white hair and sagging wrinkles furrowed my brow? At least Aurora didn't reject Tithonus, old, didn't allow him to lie there lonely in the House of Dawn... Her joy was greater that old Tithonus was alive.
Propertius, Book II.18A:5-22 Youth and Age

But no old age would lead me away from loving you, not even if I was Tithonus.
Propertius, Book II.25:1-48 Constancy and Inconstancy

The University's quantum mechanics lab smelled of pepperoni and roses. The rose scent came from the vase of flowers Sophia kept on the counter, right next to the microwave that had cooked hundreds of pizzas. She walked straight toward it the minute she and Tith walked in the door.

"Is now really the time for melted cheese and carcinogenic pepperoni?" Tith asked.

"There is no time that is not the time for microwave pizza." Sophia tapped her fingers on the counter while the pizza cooked and then pulled it out, still steaming. "Mary Mother of God, that's hot."

Tith laughed. "It amazes me that a woman who earned two PhD's by the time she was twenty-nine can't figure out the basics of heat transference."

"Spacetime is my forte, not pizza," she said, sitting on a black leather couch they'd found in the trash heap of a frat house. The springs sagged, even under her light weight, seventy-five percent of which seemed to come from her mane of dark, curly hair. With that glorious hair and her gray eyes, she looked like she would be more at home in a Romani camp than a physics lab.

The couch sat in a small room dominated by a console with several LCD screens and a wide range of keyboards, buttons, lights, levers and other signs of scientific prowess. Visitors were most impressed by the device bearing the plaque "Multiverse Manipulation Console" or MMC—a fancy name for "the thing that opens the wormhole." It looked like a small centrifuge that might generate enough power to dry a pair of jeans. Tonight, they were testing it by opening a portal to one of the many worlds predicted by quantum physics, sending a recording device through, and then, even more mind-blowing, bringing it back.

Sophia hated the clinical term "Multiverse Manipulation Console" and had named their device *Eos*, in homage to the Greek myth that had been Sophia's inspiration for a critical breakthrough. And she'd been drawn to the idea by his name. Tithonus.

It had been three years ago, and they'd been holed up in the physics lab, trying and failing, as hundreds had before them, to create enough exotic matter to generate a wormhole.

"What's up with the name Tithonus? Do you have a girlfriend named Eos?" she'd asked.

He'd looked up in shock. No one had ever picked up on the connection between his name and the myth of Eos and Tithonus. That was the moment he'd known he loved her.

"You know the myth?" he'd asked, incredulous.

She'd waved her hand as if to say, "who doesn't"? "Yeah. Eos asked Zeus for eternal life for her lover Tithonus, but forgot to ask for eternal youth. Tithonus got really old and decrepit and riddled with pain. Eventually Eos, even though she loved him desperately, took pity on him and turned him into a grasshopper." She'd taken a bite of her pizza. "So why that myth?"

He laughed. "My mother was sentimental. She foisted the idea of Eos and Tithonus's eternal love on me ever since I was a baby."

"There had to be a better way for Eos to handle it. Though, right? I mean, asking Zeus for another favor wouldn't be a good idea, but..." She'd trailed off, jumped over to her keyboard, and started typing away.

"What?" Tithonus had asked.

"Had she had any brains at all, Eos would have used the many worlds theory to find a "place" in the spacetime continuum where Tithonus could be both immortal and young," Sophia had muttered.

"Not really a thing in Greek mythology, but OK." Tith had always looked at the myth as a mildly interesting story about the origins of the grasshopper, not whatever Sophia had going on in that brilliant brain of hers.

Sophia had looked up from her computer long enough to frown at him. "Don't you get it?"

And in that one insight she found a way to make their "mad scientist" research, which rarely received any support, the most well-funded program in the history of the University. After just one meeting with potential funders, in which she implied their research might find a way to reverse aging, she and Tith had received enough funds to create the *Eos* device.

The innocuous-looking box now sat on a stand in a glass room, ready to generate enough exotic matter to open a stable wormhole. Sophia dubbed *Eos*'s home the "transporter room," despite Tith's insistence that the *Eos* didn't "beam" anyone anywhere. The room shared a glass wall with their control station, allowing them to watch the process unfold.

"All right, mad scientist. Let's do this," she said, walking toward her keyboard while cracking her knuckles and stretching her fingers. "The boot-up sequence will take ten minutes."

Tith cleared his throat. "I have something for you," he said. From his pocket, he pulled a beat-up old Seiko watch that had been in his family for generations. The face was cracked, and the band didn't clasp all the way, but if wound every day, it kept perfect time. An engraving on the back read *Lost time is never found again*. He handed it to her.

"It's my nerdy scientist way of telling you how much I've learned from you—about time, space, life, and how happy I am that you agreed to be my wife." He couldn't keep the awkwardness out of his voice. Scientists didn't usually say these kinds of things.

For once, Sophia had no smart comeback. She tucked the watch into her pocket and looked into his eyes, her own sparkling with tears.

"Remember this moment," she said. "Don't let it pass without really being here. With me. I love you and you love me, and together we're about to change the world."

He took a deep breath. "All right, my love. Shall we change the fabric of spacetime together?" He moved their intertwined hands toward the start button.

"Do we count down from ten?" she joked. But he knew they didn't need a countdown. They were now and had always been in sync. They pressed the button.

Nothing happened.

"It'll take a minute," Tith said, squeezing her hand. She nodded and kept her eyes on the video camera strapped to the *Eos* device. They both stared, as if looking away might negate the whole experiment.

After a couple minutes, Tith noticed Sophia's leg bouncing up and down, a sure sign of frustrated eagerness.

"I think something's wrong. Maybe I should—" She moved as if to leave the control room. He kept his grip on her hand, pulling her back to her seat.

"No, you're not going anywhere. If it doesn't happen in a few more minutes, we'll shut it down and try again."

"But I can just go down there and—"

"It's not safe."

"But it's obviously not working, so there's no need to worry. Stop being so stodgy."

His patience hit a breaking point. "Sophia, stop this. I get that you're eager, but even you should recognize the need for caution."

"Fine," she snapped. After another tense five minutes a light in the transporter room flickered and they leaned forward. But the video camera didn't move.

"There's got to be something wrong in there. A burned-out circuit or something. Let me just go and fix it."

Tith looked back at the *Eos* screens. None of the readings had changed. "Maybe you're right," he said, releasing her hand. "Let's try again." He moved to shut down the program. She jumped up and rushed toward the glass-walled room where the unresponsive device sat.

"Hold on," he said. "I need a minute."

His fingers raced across the keyboard, but before he could stop her, she opened the door to the transporter room and moved toward the stand in the middle.

"I think I see the problem," she called. "Looks like a fuse blew. The whole thing shut down. Dead as a doornail. It'll take at least twenty minutes to reboot." She flipped a circuit breaker on *Eos's* side.

The flash that ended his life came with no warning. In the transporter room Sophia turned toward him, looking elated, then confused, then terrified. No sounds came through the intercom and Tith saw rather than heard her scream. He tried to reboot *Eos*, but it had started cycling down. Sophia was right. Between the boot-up process and whatever had happened after they'd pressed the button, it would need to regenerate for twenty minutes before he could start it up again.

A wormhole developed behind her. She tried to run, but the gravitational pull was too intense. He realized what was about to happen and his eyes filled with tears.

"I'll open it again. Just wait for me," he wailed as he watched the gaping maw of the wormhole swallow her.

§

Tith pounded on the keyboard, almost tearing it apart in his wrath and desperation. But no, he had to keep it together. He had to let *Eos* boot-up, then recreate their exact steps. Clearly, something about hitting the switch on *Eos*'s side had changed the whole dynamic.

Once the program finished rebooting, he repeated every step with a precision that spoke to his scientific training. He let the program run for as long as it had before, waited for ten minutes, then ran toward the door to the transporter room. He wrenched it open and stumbled toward the device. Yes, it did look like a fuse had blown. He flipped the switch, felt a flood of light, and . . .

. . . that's when Sophia and a young girl appeared, mirrored against the backdrop of a swirling portal. He reached for her, but Sophia screamed at him to stay back.

"Don't step through that portal!"

He watched as the figures became more and more clear. The light and noise built to a crescendo that nearly deafened and blinded him. He raced back to the control room and shut *Eos* down just as Sophia and the little girl emerged.

Sophia looked beautiful, but she'd changed. She was older and her face reflected a sorrow and responsibility he'd never seen there before. She'd always been carefree. Now she was careworn. He moved toward her, terrified. What had happened? Why was she so much older? Who was this child with her?

She paused, her hand to her mouth, looking around and then at him. "Tith? Mary Mother of God, it worked?" The light and sun that defined Sophia came back. She threw her arms around his neck, gripping him like a woman grips a long-lost love who just come back from a dangerous journey. The little girl clung to Sophia's leg, hiccupping sobs.

"Thank God," Tith said, clasping her to him. It was the first time he'd ever thanked a deity in his life. "But, how, why...," he leaned back and took in the age-generated changes in her face. "It's been only twenty minutes."

Tears ran down Sophia's cheeks as she whispered, "It's been five years for me."

Tith dropped his arms and took a step back, unable to muster a response.

"Momma, what's happening?" The high, clear voice rang through the cold, hard lab. In struggling with the aftermath of Sophia's words, Tith had forgotten the little girl. The child looked to be about four, maybe five years old. She had dark, curly hair and curious gray eyes that in the light of the fluorescents looked almost clear. No one could mistake her for anyone but Sophia's daughter. The thought of Sophia with someone else hurt him so much he forgot about the whole spacetime mess.

"Interesting," he said. "It looks like we're not exactly the happy couple we once were." The words came out as if he were reading from a teleprompter. He didn't know whether to feel angry, confused, sad, or scared. He decided to feel all at the same time.

Instead of looking guilty, Sophia looked bemused. "Tith, this is Mena. Mena, say hello."

"Hello." With a little prodding, Mena moved out from behind her mother. Tith looked at her, trying to keep a scowl off his face. She stared back at Tith without flinching as he took in her cherubic face and wicked little smile—the smile of a tiny troublemaker. She batted some curls out of her eyes, and he noticed her strong facial structure and aristocratic nose, so unusual in such a young girl.

He froze. "She's not . . ."

"I had planned to tell you *after* our experiment worked. I thought you might come up with some ridiculous reason why I couldn't come to the lab if I told you I was pregnant."

"Are you my dad?" Mena asked, with the bluntness most people lose by the time they're ten,

Tith looked at Sophia. What could he say to that?

"Yes," Sophia said. "This is him." She whispered in Mena's ear as if sharing a secret. "What do you think?" Mena looked Tith over and shrugged.

"He's OK," she said, turning back to Sophia.

"High praise," Sophia mouthed over Mena's head.

Tith stood, staring at Mena, unable to express his devastation at not being there for her birth and young childhood, as well as his aching desire to get to know her, something that would happen only if they figured out a solution, and soon. He had no idea how time worked between these two universes.

"You have to explain everything. And quickly. How did you know when and where to find me?" he asked.

"Mena, show your father our secret weapon."

Mena pulled out the battered Seiko watch, a serious expression on her face.

"This is yours," she said. "And Momma said I shouldn't let go of it." Tith could tell she wanted him to know that she took her responsibility seriously.

"It's OK now." he said. "You did a great job." He turned toward Sophia.

"It stayed on my time?"

"Yes. It moved so slowly I thought it was broken at first. I kept winding it every day as…I don't know as a way to hold on to you. Then one day I noticed the second hand had moved, and I realized it still worked. It told me when to be at the place where the portal opened."

"So why didn't you just pull me through when you got to me?" It exasperated him that she'd chosen that time to be cautious.

"The portal goes only one way at a time. If you'd tried to reverse it without rebooting the program, I had no idea where we'd wind up, or even if we'd survive."

He groaned. He couldn't fault her reasoning on that.

"I guess we just run the program again," he said.

She nodded. He started the regeneration cycle.

As the system rebooted, Tith and Sophia stood, hands intertwined, checking and re-checking the calculations. Mena played underneath the table, humming softly to herself. When it was time, Tith turned to Sophia. "Let's get the hell out of here."

"You're right, Dad. Let's get the hell out of here," Mena mimicked.

Tith grimaced while Sophia laughed. He'd have to stop swearing in front of this bright, observant child. That would take some getting used to. He started up *Eos*, and the three of them moved to the transporter room. Once inside they clung to each other.

"The pull is powerful," Sophia said. "If we lose contact, don't panic. Just stay in the portal." He nodded, although he planned to stay glued to them both.

They waited through an interminable ten minutes, then Sophia hit the switch. Tith felt a flood of light pour around him and his family. He almost shook with joy. He was going home.

"Momma, I forgot the watch." Mena's tremulous voice rose in the increasing rush of wind. The wormhole began to glow, reversing its polarity. He felt Mena pull away, going back toward the lab.

"No!" Sophia screamed.

"But Momma, you told me to keep it safe," Mena wailed.

"Mena, no," Sophia screeched, her voice fading. "Leave it. Tith, grab her." But Mena was already turning, preparing to run toward where she'd left the watch on the floor under one of the tables.

Tith didn't consciously make any choices. All he knew was that he had to stop her from moving forward, and the stubborn child, who had already come loose from Sophia's grasp, would not leave without the watch. He dashed to the table, grabbed the watch and threw it into Mena's hand. Then he raced back.

But before he reached the portal, he noticed it shifting, fracturing a bit. It didn't look like it had before. Pure dread flooded him. What was the problem?

The answer hit him with the force of gravity itself. The portal would stay open and become unstable as long as the program was running. He ran to the control center, knowing that he had to shut down the program before the portal would close, and knowing what it would cost him. That's what he'd done before.

"Come on," he heard Sophia shout. She reached out her hand, and he almost wept with relief when he saw her fingers grasp Mena's wrist. His daughter's wrist. He watched as Mena moved through the rapidly closing gateway. He watched Sophia's tear-stained face fade away. He watched all this from the wrong side.

§

Tith had always wondered what it felt like to hit rock bottom, to be at the end of one's rope, to experience any other cliché of loss.

Now he knew. It felt like nothing. Every ounce of emotion left him and he stood rigid, clutching the edge of the console for support. Only the feel of the cold, hard metal assured him he was still alive.

When his emotions returned, he picked up Sophia's vase of flowers and threw it across the room.

Should I give up? Would Sophia give up?

He knew the answer. She would never give up and she would be furious if he did. She would find a way to come back. Or to send someone else back if, God forbid, she died before she could get to him.

His eyes landed on the remote for the microwave. Thank God for Sophia and her pizza.

A remote. I need to build a remote. Something I can use to shutdown Eos while we're in the portal.

He turned on the regeneration cycle. He had no idea how time moved on the other side and he had to figure this out—fast.

§

Time, like most things, is in the eye of the beholder. Logically, it should pass evenly. The human race has agreed that seconds, minutes and hours measure our movement together, as a species, through the spacetime continuum. That days, months and years measure the aging of our bodies and minds. But after he started *Eos* again, the ten minutes he waited until the wormhole opened seemed like an eternity.

When the portal finally opened, a stunning middle-aged woman came through. She wore her age well, resisting the urge to color her hair or wear too much make-up. She'd piled her long brown curls up into a bun, with streaks of gray that matched her eyes slithering through. She was definitely more than five years older than the last time he'd seen her.

After he shut *Eos* down, he ran into the transporter room, then stopped, unsure whether to hug this stranger.

"How long?" he whispered.

"Eighteen years," Sophia said. Tears coursed down her face, through wrinkles that hadn't been there the last time he saw her. He came close enough to wipe away her tears and she pulled him to her, sobbing.

"I can't believe you're fifty-two," he said, cradling her to his chest. "You still look twenty-nine to me."

She looked up at him, and the smile that emerged through her tears brought back the image of the woman he loved.

"You'll need to learn to lie a lot better if you're going to talk about the looks of your much older wife. People will call me a cougar," she said.

"And people will call me a genius for making such a brilliant match," he countered. "It killed me to leave you in the portal last time. But I had to shut down *Eos* from this side." He picked up the homemade remote and showed it to her. "But that sure as hell isn't going to happen again. I made this."

"You are a genius. An actual genius!" Then she smiled wickedly,

"As am I." She waved a device that looked like a cable TV remote in front of him.

He laughed. They'd always been in sync, and here was further proof.

"This is going to work, isn't it?" he asked.

She grinned. "How can it not?"

A small part of him shuddered at the words. She put her hand on his cheek.

"Don't worry. It *will* work." She sat down on the loveseat and crossed her legs. "Now, while we wait for the regeneration cycle, I better show you some pictures of your family." She pulled a stack of photos from her pocket.

"Photographs? Actual pieces of paper? You still have those where, or when, you are?"

"Yes," she said dryly. "They're very 'in' right now. Very retro. Like sheepskin would have been in our time."

He laughed. Her voice and words sounded the same as when she was twenty-nine years old. If he closed his eyes he could see her as she was. Suddenly he was desperate to know the family.

"How's Mena?" he asked.

"Mena's doing great. Almost as much of a hellion as her mother, although with a touch of the gravitas of her father. She's married now, and—"

"—Married? At ..." he did the math. "At twenty-two?" he sputtered.

Sophia laughed. "She's grown up seeing how quickly life can pass you by. She didn't want to wait to get married," she paused. "Or have kids."

"Kids?"

"Yes, a little girl named Zoe. The two of us being grandparents is a sobering thought, isn't it?"

"Not sobering. Amazing."

They sat close together on the love seat, touching—always touching—while she showed him the family. Their children and grandchildren. Students in her college classes. A trip to Costa Rica. Her volunteering at an animal shelter. They talked about what they'd do when he became part of that life. How they'd become that snooty academic couple who wear tweed and go to pretentious cocktail parties. How they'd embarrass their daughter and granddaughter with their public displays of affection.

He wondered if she'd edited out images of a boyfriend in the tales of her life. In eighteen years, it wasn't to be unexpected. The thought made him ask a question he hadn't expected to ask.

"Why do you do it? Why do you keep searching for me?"

She looked confused, then incredulous.

"You know why. I search for you because I love you. I've always loved you and I will always love you. No rip in spacetime is going to change that."

He pulled her to him, finally understanding what his mother tried to teach him about Eos and Tithonus.

§

After starting *Eos* for the third time, they stood in the transporter room, both gripping their remotes and each other.

"This better work," she said. "I have no idea how long the next cycle will be, but I will draw the line at dating a man more than ten years my junior."

When the ten minutes passed, Tith hit the switch on the console. Back came the flood of light he'd felt from before. The air around them started to shift and they clung to each other as power built around them. Tith punched the remote and the world on the other side of the wormhole started to materialize. A woman, clearly of Sophia's lineage, stood hand-in-hand with a young girl. Mena? Mena's daughter? He had no idea, given the vagaries of time between his lab and the world. He didn't care.

Just as he started to exhale the breath he felt as though he'd been holding for years, that other world, the one he wanted to get to so desperately, started to fracture. Tiny fragments of it flashed out of existence as he and Sophia came closer. He looked over his shoulder and saw that the gateway in the lab wasn't closing. Pulling his hand from Sophia's, he pounded on the remote with his fist.

"What's happening?" Her voice sounded tinny, like when he used to play telephone with two cans and a string when he was young.

"It's not working," he screamed. He grabbed her remote and pounded it as well.

"Neither is this one."

Now he knew how Odysseus felt, caught between the Scylla and Charybdis. Except in his case no course would lead him through to the other side. And if he tried the other side could be destroyed. He could pull her back with him. She would forgive him for that, he knew. But they couldn't know how much time would pass until they could try again. Sophia had a family she needed to take care of. He had nothing.

When he stepped away from her, he felt as though he were being sucked into the mouth of some sea creature, swirling faster and faster away from those he loved. Tears streamed down her face.

"No," she mouthed. "Please."

"You've got to go. Mena is waiting for you. Zoe is waiting for you. Go back to our family." He ran back into the control room and began shutting down the program manually.

The portal began to swallow her up. She kept reaching for him and screaming his name. He saw her posture change as she gave up and shrunk back, letting herself fall through the swirling vortex.

"See you soon," she mouthed, as she disappeared.

"I'll be here," he whispered.

§

When the light flashed again in the transporter room, an old woman staggered out. He'd thought he was prepared to see her in any state, or perhaps not at all. He was wrong. Nothing could prepare him to see the woman he loved clad in someone else's skin. She lifted her head wearily.

"Tith," she croaked, looking up at him. He saw her beautiful gray eyes, buried beneath decades of life. He entered the transporter room and reached for her, saddened by her frailness.

"How long this time?" he asked, resigned to whatever she would say. She didn't try to ease him into the truth.

"Forty years." She was now ninety-two years old.

They stood in silence for a moment, beyond weeping. Following his first instinct, he tried a joke to ease the sense of despair smothering him.

"So that makes you a really, really old cougar."

Something not quite like a smile, more like an absence of debilitating pain, appeared on her face. Her beautiful smile had left her. Whether it was the years or the tragedy of their love, he'd never know.

"You'll be happy to know I've put the years to good use. I know how to get you out," she said. "Apparently, the signals from the remotes can't move through the wormhole. So, I discovered a code I can build in that will shut the program down automatically."

He should have felt elated at this news. Or even relieved. Instead, he felt devastated. He'd missed out on an entire lifetime with her. It didn't matter anymore.

"I'm looking forward to watching you age a little when you get back," she said. But her voice sounded sad, like she knew, given her age, she wouldn't get to see much of that.

He took a deep breath. "OK, show me what we need to do."

She hobbled with him into the control room and smiled.

"I keep thinking how miserable you must be stuck in here for so long, until I realize it's been only an hour or so for you." She coughed, a raking cough that spoke of a long-term illness. He reached out and she waved his hands away.

"Don't worry, I'm fine. I've been dying to get these arthritic hands on this keyboard." She sat at her old chair and checked the time left in the reboot process. Fifteen minutes.

"I'll need your help with the updates to the *Eos* device itself." She nodded toward the transporter room. "Once we get this calibrated, I'll be able to tell you how to reconfigure the circuits. While we wait, I need to show you more about your family."

She pulled out a small round device the size of a coin and pressed it. A holographic image appeared. "This—" she showed an image of a little girl with a rounded, soft face, dimples and deep brown eyes "—is Sophia. She's your great-granddaughter."

He stared. "So, Mena…"

"Sophia is Mena's granddaughter. Mena's daughter Zoe named Sophia after me. She said she wanted a Sophia in her life after I'm gone."

"She's adorable," he said. "How old is she?"

"Eight. She has your smarts and my complete lack of appropriateness. Fortunately, she also has some of Mena's common sense."

As they waited, she showed him several lives' worth of images. Zoe's college graduation. A dog named Arthur. A trip to Disneyland with a curly-haired little girl. Thanksgivings. Christmases. A Fourth of July in Washington, DC. For ten minutes, Sophia's life flashed before his eyes—Zoe's wedding. Mena's fiftieth birthday party. Her own seventy-fifth birthday. Any trepidation he might have had at spending the next few years with this older, alien Sophia disappeared. Their lives had been so ravaged by time. Now he would be getting some back.

The console beeped, indicating that the reboot had finished. He looked at her expectantly.

"What's the plan?"

"I've developed a script that will give us a longer time between shutdown of the program and shutdown of the portal. After you flip the switch on *Eos*, I'll have time to get to the transporter room."

"I think maybe I can get back to the transporter room faster than you," he argued.

"Yes, but do you know the math behind what I'm proposing?"

He shrugged. "I'm sure I can follow it."

"In ten minutes? I think not. But don't worry. I'll have plenty of time to get to the portal."

The whole set-up made him nervous, but he figured she'd had forty years to figure this out, while he'd had twenty minutes. He went into the transporter room and waited for her signal.

"Alright," she said. "Let her rip!"

He flipped the switch, and felt the light, heard the wind, and saw Sophia…not moving. She smiled at him sadly. In a flash, he realized the awful truth.

Sophia's voice came over the speaker. "Tith, my love. I can't risk another technological failure." He could see tears in her eyes. "I've had my life. Now you need to have yours."

§

Tith opened his eyes and saw light. Not the flash of the wormhole he just came through—but softer, almost like a fluorescent. He was in a soft bed, covered in a blue quilt that came up to his neck. Looking around, he saw nothing more mysterious than a regular bedroom with a dresser on one wall, a bookcase on another, and a rocking chair decorated in tasteful shades of dark blue and tan. The scent of roses and vanilla lingered in the air.

A woman stood at the window with her back to him. Her dark, wild hair floated around her like a halo, and he could tell that she was young and strong and whole. His heart stuttered as he concluded that this was his Sophia, and somehow—somehow—they have restored the timeline. He sat up and tried to get out of the bed, overwhelmed with the love he felt.

The woman turned, and he saw she was not Sophia. She was younger, maybe in her late teens or early twenties. Her eyes were a deep, rich brown, instead of gray-green, and her hair was tinged with auburn. Her face was more rounded, giving it a softness that came from neither Sophia nor him. It was all her own.

"Who are you?" he breathed.

"I'm Sophia." The sleeve of her shirt fell away from her arm, and he noticed an ancient watch circling her wrist. She smelled of the rose scent he'd always associated with his Sophia. But this wasn't her.

"I don't understand."

"I'm Sophia," she repeated. Her smile dazzled, but it was different than his Sophia's. She had dimples, making it less wild. "Zoe's daughter. Your great-granddaughter."

He hadn't realized until now how he'd let hope creep into his heart. Hope that his trip through the wormhole would set everything right. The years washed over him, drowning him, leaving him unable to even gasp for air. Images of Sophia flashed through his mind. Images of their life together, had they not tried to mess with time. Their wedding. Mena's birth. A set of rocking chairs on a porch.

The images crushed his hope and him along with it. He fell back on the bed, and this Sophia, his great-granddaughter, grasped both his hands.

"Grandfather—" She saw his expression at the word. "Tith." Tears flooded her eyes, and he could see her disappointment. He realized she'd hoped he would be happy to meet her. To know her. He tried to smile and she smiled back, brushing a lock of hair from her face. The gesture was so much like his Sophia that his heart broke all over again.

"She left a letter for you." She handed him a piece of paper. It was browned with age, and the writing faded. But he could still see Sophia's strong, flowing script in the words. He could hear her voice, both serious and lighthearted, telling him of her love.

Tith,

When you read this, you'll know of the choice I made. If you know me at all, it shouldn't surprise you.

I've had my life. You must have yours. And try to live, my love. Really live. Don't lock yourself in your cluttered office, flipping through Bullfinch's translation of Greek myths and the latest quantum physics journal. I know it seems positively Appalachian for you to have children and grandchildren older than you, but spend time with them. Get to know your family. They are our bond that will last through past, present and future.

Don't be sad for me. I had a good life. You were always there.

Love—

Sophia

Epilogue

He winds the watch, more out of habit than anything else now. Thirty minutes have passed in Sophia's world. He is where the portal will open, waiting to return, having lived the full life she wanted him to live.

In the last forty-five years, he has been to school plays and chaperoned high school dances. He helped his grandchildren learn to tie their shoes and ride a bike. He tutored them in physics, until their teachers called and told him he was confusing them. He spoke at their school assemblies—the man lost in time— making them instant celebrities.

As he grew older, he scared the neighborhood kids off the front porch and complained in public places that the music was too loud. He went to restaurants for the early bird special and insisted on having his senior discount at every opportunity. He buried both his daughter Mena and his granddaughter Zoe. He started going to church, not out of any new-found belief in a higher power, but to gather evidence of the possibility. It's not something he knows how to test, but he's sure he will eventually.

He was with his great granddaughter Sophia for the births of each of her three children, Christopher, Tithonus and Theresa. He told her she didn't need to saddle anyone with his name, but she insisted. Her one daughter, Theresa, calls him "Pop-Pop Tith," and at seven, already has the same sunny, wicked disposition as all the women in her family. She holds a special place in his heart, even as she grows older and out of the habits of her youngest years, when she would beg him to tell her bedtime stories.

Her favorite was the fable of the Grasshopper and the Dawn.

"That's not a good myth for little girls," he'd say, teasing her. "Don't you want to hear about how Ariadne and Theseus escaped the Minotaur?" He always left out the part where the Minotaur ate people.

"No! Grasshopper and the Dawn, Pop-Pop." He'd sigh, and tuck the quilt around her neck and he'd say:

"Have you heard the myth of the Grasshopper and the Dawn? Eos, goddess of the dawn, fell in love with a mortal named Tithonus. Wanting to be with him forever, Eos begged her father Zeus to grant her beloved immortality. Zeus loved his daughter and granted her wish."

"Do they get to be together forever, Pop-Pop?" She asked that every time, even though she knew the answer.

"Just listen, little girl," he'd say. "But Eos had forgotten to ask for eternal youth for her Tithonus. She watched him age, but he would never die. As he grew older she took pity on him and turned him into a grasshopper. He sat at her hearth, loving her always. And she loved him. Their love did not die with age or the passage of time. It lasts to this day, tinged with loss. Her tears can still be seen in the morning dew. And in the early hours, the grasshopper comes out to drink them."

When he'd had to say goodbye to Theresa, to tell her he would be leaving and not coming back, she'd sobbed as only little girls can sob, hopelessly and breathlessly. Like her whole world had been crushed by this news.

"But Theresa," he'd said. "I'm returning to your great-great Grandmother. We'll be together. Just like the Grasshopper and the Dawn."

"Really?" she'd whispered.

"Yes, love. And I can't wait to tell her all about you."

And it's true. He can't wait. He'd hoped to live to this day. To the day he would find Sophia again. And today, just hours before dawn, a bright light shines, and he knows she has found him.

Stephanie's speculative fiction seeks to blend humor and social commentary in a way that leaves the reader both amused and contemplative (though she'll settle or one or the other). Her work has appeared in outlets such as *Andromeda Spaceways* magazine and the anthologies *One Star Reviews of the Afterlife, Enter the Apocalypse*, and *As Told by Things*. Her romantic comedy, *Across the Aisle*, from Entangled Publishing, was released in May 2022. Stephanie holds an MFA in genre fiction from Western Colorado University. She lives and works in Washington, DC, where she tries to make the world a better place by facilitating effective grassroots advocacy. It's going really well.

The Transfer of Venus

Doug Engstrom

I fly the Venus Atmosphere Penetration Explorer, the only vehicle that can ferry humans between the high-altitude research station in the planet's upper atmosphere and the surface. It carries only two people, meaning that for this mission, I will have two jobs: command pilot and CEO babysitter. I have extensive training, experience and enthusiasm for the first job; for the second, not so much.

It didn't help that when we met, our fearless leader's first reaction was some vulgar quip about being confined in a tight space with a redhead in a vehicle designated as a "penetrator." I kept my face neutral, but when he asked for my first name, I told him I didn't mind being called "Commander." There are some advantages to being one of only two qualified VAPE pilots left after last quarter's cuts, especially since the other one was puking his guts out down in sick bay, and Mr. Trask was desperate to get to the surface.

Right now, our bathysphere-slung-under-a-zeppelin craft has been descending for two hours, and Trask is bored. He squirms in his seat, and I imagine the old mattress smell that permeates the vehicle is getting to him. He doesn't understand the displays, and the view out the window is constant, boiling clouds. Hypnotic, but not enough to keep him occupied. VAPE is well-behaved today, almost like she knows she's performing for the boss, and I have little to do during our descent except watch the altimeter and think.

It would be a quiet descent – if Trask hadn't started a monologue, rattling off details about the VAPE and the data she collected, as if he'd spent the last year or so living in a hostile planet's atmosphere and I was newly arrived from a mansion near Malibu, instead of the other way around. He's wrong about quite a few details. Does he remember things incorrectly or did the research teams lie to him to keep him off their backs? I just met him yesterday, and I'm already willing to say almost anything to make him shut up, so no judgment on the teams if that's what they did.

It is just barely possible that one person might deserve credit for terraforming Venus, and thereby have some semi-reasonable claim to the planet, but if there is such a person, it is definitely not the smug little fucker sharing my control cabin. But the purpose of today's flight is to get him to the surface so he can step on the ground, plant a flag, and claim the place for his little private equity company, of which he is both the CEO and the largest stockholder. To be fair, it's the only entity that has done much to get humans out into the solar system since sea level rise picked up and most national governments decided saving coastal cities was a higher priority than exploring the cosmos. His company is also the organization that pays me and built VAPE, which is, without a doubt, the coolest aircraft anyone has ever flown on any planet.

VAPE can float like a dirigible in the Venusian atmosphere, but she can also withstand as much pressure as a shallow-water submarine. Her hydrogen-burning, high-bypass turbofan engines can push her up to 300 knots on a good day, and her reinforced envelope and supporting framework will take it. My boss may be four different kinds of asshole, but his advanced materials division does good work. VAPE can swap through five different configurations to handle everything from weather observation to delivering remote-control rovers to the surface, making her the perfect tool for exploring Venus. I'll always be proud to have flown her, regardless of the purpose she serves. How many people do you know who have an endorsement for flight in the Venusian atmosphere on their pilot's license?

We break through the final cloud deck, and the surface comes into view. Everything is bathed in an eerie yellow glow, as if the light is coming through a beige sheet. I pick out a brighter area that looks like it's probably where the sun is, but it's hard to tell. Below us—nothing but slick gray rock. The wind shifts, and I point us into it and throttle up. The wind shifts again, and a liquid sheet strikes our window with a resounding *thwack*. It takes the wiper blades a full two strokes to clear it.

"Oh, it's the rain." He peers out the window. "Think there's any chance it will let up?"

I keep my mouth shut and study the main navigation screen, but in my head, I explain it to him using the most condescending tone imaginable.

For about a hundred years, biohacked blue-green algae, seeded by the European Space Agency during better times, has worked to produce this rain. The one-celled organisms have made their way down through the atmosphere by layers, converting the carbon dioxide in one layer into oxygen and organic compounds until the layer releases enough heat that water vapor condenses into rain, which falls into the next layer, cooling it. Once the next layer is cool enough, the algae occupies it and repeats the process until we have what we see below—liquid flowing on the Venusian surface for the first time in 750 million years. Along with a rainstorm that wouldn't let up for another couple decades or so. Somehow, the man who thinks he should own the entire planet didn't know that.

He probably doesn't know the liquid is basically high-grade industrial acid, either.

Where the liquid collects, it absorbs my craft's radar pulse and displays as a dark line or shape that stands out against the bright reflection from surrounding rock, just like water back on Earth. This makes it easy to find my landmark—a distinctive point where three rivers come together like the tines of a pitchfork—and compare it to our flight plan. Based on that, I adjust our heading, bump the throttle up a little more, and continue our descent. We're on a course that will take us to the lowest point on the planet, a place that will eventually become the deepest trench in the largest sea on Venus.

My comm crackles. "VAPE 1, this is Venus Control. Do you read?"

"Affirmative, Venus Control. This is VAPE 1. What's up?"

"VAPE 1, that little storm forming to your south has taken a turn your direction and looks like it's spooling up into a Cat 20 hurricane. You must now begin your ascent in one hour. Repeat, you must begin ascent in no more than one, repeat one, hour. Do you copy?"

"Roger that, Venus Control. We are about…" I study the radar image and do some math in my head. "…twenty minutes from target. We will begin ascent in one hour or less. VAPE 1 out."

I keep VAPE's nose pitched down and vent gas to reduce our buoyancy.

"Just an hour?" He's whining.

"Less than that. It's still about a twenty-minute trip and we have to get anchored."

He looks petulant.

I point to the ceiling. "That reinforced balloon we're riding is pretty tough, but it won't stand up to 500 mile per hour winds. We want to be safely in the troposphere when it hits."

Incredibly, he looks unconvinced, but before he can say more, VAPE picks up the radio beacon that marks our landing site, and I adjust our course based on that.

Would this be any better if I were ferrying an heir of Andrew Clark? Clark had the foresight to take advantage of a once-in-a-millennia planetary alignment, an oddball regulatory loophole, and one big-ass fusion pulse motor to shove Saturn's moon Rhea toward Venus. The resulting off-center impact spun the planet fast enough to give it a 30-hour day and a respectable magnetic field, while the icy bits supplied more water than Venus had ever had. But would his great-great-grandkids be any better than the entitled twatwaffle in the seat next to me? Probably not. In any case, their potential claims had all sunk into the swamps of bankruptcy litigation more than twenty years before I was born.

My musings cease when I spot the target—the ultimate end point for all the flowing liquid on the planet, and the point from which,

The Transfer of Venus 39

according to precedents invoked by Trask's lawyers, he will claim ownership of all lands draining into this lake by standing on its bank. This is the same legal trick invoked by explorers who claimed huge tracts of the Americas by being the first European to set foot near a river's mouth. Apparently a couple centuries of warfare and genocide aren't enough to disturb a legal precedent.

I adjust our flight path and begin our final descent. Trask gazes out over his soon-to-be-domain, his eyes shining. Why shouldn't he be excited? In exchange for the relatively modest cost of setting up the high-altitude research station and building VAPE, he is in the right place at the right time to claim an entire world for himself. And I'm helping him do it.

I get us securely anchored to a rock right on the lake's edge and complete the landing checklist. The acid rain patters on our craft like applause from a distant audience. I check in. "Venus Control, VAPE1. We have landed."

"Roger that, VAPE1. Cap says, 'Get in, get the job done, then get the hell out.'"

At this point, my job is to get my companion outside and then use our court-approved, tamper-proof cameras to get time-stamped pics of him on the Venusian surface.

One small step for a man; one giant leap for that man's net worth.

"Affirmative, Venus Control. We will release in no more than thirty minutes."

He's got his environment suit halfway on when he sticks his head back into the cockpit. "I think you should come out, too."

"That's not protocol." He does not seem to understand this is code for, *That is an unbelievably bad idea,* so I elaborate. "I'm supposed to suit up and stay with the ship while you go out and stake your claim. That way, if anything goes wrong, I'm in place to get you safely out."

"Protocol." He says it the way you'd say the name of a bankrupt company or other object of disgust. "It's just us down here. We can do whatever we want."

It never occurred to me that he might regard rules intended to keep us alive on a hostile, alien planet as fussy bureaucratic restrictions. Maybe that's what happens when your staff, your government, or your business partners save your ass with monotonous regularity—you regard your survival and success as a function of natural law.

He gives me that excited-little-boy expression that the press loves. "C'mon, it'll be fun."

I give him the Mom Look. "I'm not here to have fun, I'm here to do a job."

He looks sullen. "Well, I'm the person you're doing the job for, and I want you to come out."

So, despite the time pressure and the safety concerns, I enter the crew compartment and suit up. We're both sitting in the airlock when he comes clean on the real reason. "Will you take a picture of me stepping down from the ship?" He gestured toward the window, where we could see the camera on a boom protruding from the hull. "The picture that one takes will look like some half-assed selfie."

So that's the deal. I'm risking both our lives and mission failure because he wants a cooler-looking photo. Without waiting for my answer, he hands me his extra camera. While he normally believes that redundancy is a Latin term for "Why am I paying for this?" the lawyers have prevailed upon him to bring five cameras to the surface—two out on the boom, the two handhelds we've got with us now, and a spare handheld back in the locker, ready for use if things go sideways with the ones we're carrying. All with features that will make their images irrefutable, date and time stamped evidence when presented in court. I take the proffered camera and put it in my pressure suit's left exterior pocket.

I also start to think through what he's just asked me to do. There's enough riding on this I need to be absolutely clear. "So, you're ordering me to go out first and then get a picture of you stepping onto the surface?"

He looks peeved, like I'm the one being a jerk. "Yes, that's what I'm telling you to do."

So yes, I did notice. And no, he did not. I guess once you get used to treating other people as meaningless objects, there are some things you stop seeing. And once you realize you're being treated as a meaningless object, it can cause you to redefine certain concepts—organizational loyalty, for example. The lock's outer door opens, and I make my way out, ass-backwards into the acid downpour. He sticks his head out the door, and his voice comes over the comm. "Get it from a low angle."

I sigh, but then I kneel in the semi-liquid sludge of deceased algae and fumble with my camera. I get a couple pictures of my foot—and you can tell it's my foot, because "Jenkins" is right there on the toes—before I'm situated to give him his hero shot. He steps down from the airlock, getting into a position that makes him look like he's posing for a founder's statue. I get the picture. I get several. He's pleased with them.

We unbundle and activate a couple instrument packages—OK, I'm the one who does that—and we extract the company flag from a cargo pocket and schlepp down to the lake's edge. I test the light by taking a few pictures of myself on the lakeshore, then I take some of him, again in poses ready to be cast in bronze. Just to make sure, we get a few shots using his camera and then we plant the flag in a spot that looks like it won't immediately be covered by the rapidly-filling lake, grab a few rock samples, and hightail it back to the ship.

It's a rough ride on the way up. The wind smacks us around a little, and we get struck by lightning. Twice. Fortunately, VAPE is tough as well as beautiful, and we arrive at the high-altitude station in good shape.

§

When we unload back at the research station, I wait until no one is paying attention, and then swap my camera with the spare. This puts the camera with the pictures showing my toes on Venus with the other extra gear we didn't use on the trip. I then plug the spare into an overpowered charger that fries it before placing it in the tamper-proof box mandated by the legal department. When the damage is discovered, it's blamed on the lightning strikes we took on the way up. He waxes despondent about losing the "good shots" of him descending from the airlock, but never becomes suspicious.

He remains oblivious even when we board the *Endeavor* for the trip back to Earth. Despite the photographic evidence for my toes hitting Venus first, it's not going to do me any good unless I can get it into my possession. I tell his ranking PR flunky how much I'd like the expedition's spare camera as a souvenir, and she seizes on the suggestion as the chance for a small victory in her perpetual uphill battle to humanize Trask's image. Trask presents me with the camera during a party attended by the entire crew and livestreamed back to Earth. He says he's chosen that memento because he pressed me into service as the expedition photographer, and I doubt he or anyone watching understands why I laugh so hard at that joke.

§

Even though I had a valid claim under rules his lawyers established, and even though he gave me the evidence as a gift in front of witnesses, I knew I couldn't fight his legal team all by myself. So, I signed over both my claim and the supporting evidence to a foundation that says it intends to make Venus part of mankind's common heritage and run it on a cooperative basis. They're idealists, and more important, they're ready to duke it out with Trask in ways I am not.

The foundation has raised more money for this fight than you might expect. The most public donors are people who get behind the dream of Venus as a cooperative Eden, while the biggest donations come from Trask's rivals, who view screwing up his Venus claim as a strategic move. However, the largest group of donors is people who want to show Trask and people like him their middle fingers.

Honestly, I probably identify with that group the most.

So far, we've gotten through a blizzard of pretrial motions concerning everything from accusations of fraud to arcane points of Renaissance property law. We also learned that in the opinion of the US Ninth Circuit Court, "photographers don't count" isn't a legal argument. I may not live long enough to see how the litigation plays out, but the algae will continue to do its work, and by the time we finally decide who really owns it, Venus may be ready for us.

And maybe by then, we'll be ready for it.

In the course of his life, Doug has failed in an attempt to become a missile launch officer and an aircraft navigator. He succeeded in running a base newspaper on the Upper Peninsula of Michigan and has bicycled across the state of Iowa twice. He wrote *Corporate Gunslinger*, which was published by HarperVoyager in 2020. He lives near Des Moines with his wife, Catherine Engstrom.

Edgar's Foxes

George Galuschak

Cynthia Peck said – "You can have the job. If you want it."

"Why me?" Lisa asked. The Panera mirrored the city – old and run down. Early April, and the Christmas decorations were still up.

"Because I liked your last book," Cynthia said.

"I don't work fast," Lisa said. Cynthia didn't look like her father, Edgar Peck, at all. Except she did. Something in the eyes, maybe, or the way she talked.

"That's why I chose you," Cynthia said. "I don't want some quickie book. I want people to remember our story."

"How much access are we talking?" Lisa asked.

"My father had no friends, so I don't think you'll have much luck there. You can talk to me all you want. I have kids. They're off-limits. As in, don't even mention I have them." Cynthia tapped the edge of her plastic cup, smeared with bright red lipstick.

"Can I interview your ex?" Lisa asked.

"If you can talk to the dead, sure." Cynthia tittered.

"How much editorial control do you want?"

Cynthia shrugged. "Write what you want. I don't care."

"Why not? If someone was writing about my life, I'd want a say in it."

"You're writing about my father's life." Cynthia had the longest nails Lisa had ever seen. The off-white polish on them was scuffed and peeling. "This is about him. Not me. Oh, one other thing."

"What's that?"

"I won't go back to my dad's house." Cynthia tore off another strip of napkin. Rolled it into a little ball. Dropped it on the table, where it sat with all the others. "So do you want the job?"

And Lisa said – "Yes."

§

After her interview with Cynthia Peck, Lisa checked into the Motel 6 outside of Scranton. She always followed the same ritual. Flush the toilet. Put the overnight bag in the tub. Check the mattress for bedbugs. Throw the blanket cover on the floor. Call Jack.

"I got the job," she said.

"Don't sound so excited," Jack told her.

"You haven't heard what the job is yet."

"It can't be worse than the last one," he said. "Can it?"

"His name was Edgar Peck. He lived with his wife and daughter in a suburb outside Scranton. He was a bus driver for 34 years. After he retired and his wife died, he started up a YouTube Channel. Give him something to do, all that. He fed the local foxes. Called himself The Fox Whisperer."

"Next you're going to tell me he was a serial killer," Jack said.

"Bingo." Lisa sat on the bed.

"Wait. He was?"

"Yeah. He liked teenage boys. According the police records, three or four vanished every year. He picked them off like cherries. The cops thought the kids were runaways." Lisa kept her voice even.

"When did they catch him?" Jack asked.

"Technically, they never did. He got dementia. His daughter put him in a nursing home. He started talking. Boy, did he ever. Went into enough detail to get the state cops and feds involved. He'd been doing it for over twenty years."

"Are you fucking kidding me?" Jack couldn't keep the disgust out of his voice.

"I don't kid, dear. This is my job." Silence on the other end. "Now his daughter wants me to ghost-write a book about Daddy. Says there's no strings attached."

Edgar's Foxes

"Sounds like a load of fun," Jack said after a while.

"Gotta go." Lisa sensed two things coming on – a migraine and a fight. She could avoid the second. "I'll call tomorrow. Love you."

§

The fox didn't look too good. Skinny. Missing patches of fur on its back. It limped up to the patio doors that led to the backyard deck. Stood up on its hind legs. Looked at Lisa, who'd spent a long day at Edgar's old house.

One of Edgar's foxes, except that wasn't possible. After the old man went away, neighbors complained about stray foxes walking up to their back doors and patios begging for food. Gawkers came from all over, eager to see the animals. The town hired a pest control expert to round up the foxes. That was a decade ago. Did foxes live that long? This one looked young.

Lisa peered out onto the backyard deck. Gasped. A naked boy squatted there, on all fours. The boy had long oily black hair that trailed down his back and shoulders. She could see the red welts on his bare chest. Black hair covered his eyes.

Lisa pulled the curtains shut. 6:35 p.m., still daylight. She picked up her phone and dialed.

"You've seen them, I guess," Cynthia Peck said.

"You mean the foxes?"

"No. Not the foxes. Which one did you see?"

"The boy with black hair." Lisa had seen police photographs of the hidden sub-cellar, so it was possible.

"Ah, Peter. They show up in my back yard, you know," Cynthia said. She lived in Florida.

"How often?" Lisa asked.

"Often enough." Cynthia laughed. "But I'm free now. Thank you."

"The deal's off," Lisa said, and then disconnected. When she peeked through the curtains the boy with black hair was gone. She thought about calling Jack or the police. In the end, she made a run for it, sprinting past the For Sale sign to her rent-a-car.

§

"The deal's still on," Harry said. The phone connection was clear, so Lisa hadn't misheard her agent.

"What are you talking about?" Early evening, and Lisa was ready to go. She'd spent the day following her close encounter sitting in her motel room waiting for her flight home.

"Cynthia's publisher still wants you to write the book."

"I can't work with that woman," Lisa said.

"You don't have to," Harry said. "She killed herself last night."

"Shit. I talked to her on the phone yesterday."

"Well, she obviously wasn't a happy person." Harry sighed. "You've heard the stories, right?"

"Which ones? There's a lot of them," Lisa said.

"There were whispers that Cindy knew all about what her dad was doing. And that she helped him do it."

Lisa recalled Cynthia's words – *I have kids*. Her gorge rose.

"Do you think it might've been true?" she whispered.

"How should I know? Think about it, is all I'm saying," Harry told her. "You might – "

Lisa dropped her phone onto the dirty carpet. Sat very, very still. Heard it, again. Something, moving stealthily in the motel room's bathroom.

She scooped up her phone. Stepped out into the damp, wet air, leaving her bags and shoes behind. Two foxes sat on the parking lot's edge. They watched her, their eyes glowing like yellow nickels.

Lisa fast-walked down the walkway and slipped into her rental. Checked the back seat. When she glanced into the rear-view mirror, more foxes sat at the lot's edge. At least ten or twenty. Hard to tell.

She gunned the rental and screeched out of the parking lot, Cynthia's last words echoing in her head – *do you want the job?*

And her answer – *yes*.

George Galuschak is a librarian and speculative fiction writer who lives in New Jersey. His short fiction has appeared in a number of venues, including *Strange Horizons, Escape Pod,* and *Lore.* He attended the Viable Paradise and Taos Toolbox writing workshops, and worked in the gaming industry, where he wrote for Zombicide and Dark Age, a miniature skirmish board game. Mr. Galuschak has an M.F.A. in Popular Fiction from Seton Hill University. He is currently working on a novel, just like every other writer on Earth.

Apartment 2B

Ransom Noble

The building stretched into the distance, with trees inside and an entire greenhouse with exotic plants and animals to populate an entire world. Zircon thought ze owned the building and much of the surrounding areas. Ze preferred to keep just one apartment within the building, though Zircon could be found anywhere.

In apartment 2B, Zircon kept zir domain in a corner of one greenhouse, the most exotic and wonderful of them all. In this tiny spot, the fruit trees each had a branch that reached into the space as well as room for a small number of pets.

Many of the other spirits wandered through all of the apartments and free spaces, and we made ourselves known to the occupants. Each had a different story, an origin that brought a flavor to the world they created inside. Each of us had our favorites, and also the ones that simply needed to have eyes on them.

I lived in Zircon's apartment. I'm the dragon spirit, Lucy. I have free range of all the beautiful spaces that are only kept here, and all of Zircon's attention is occasionally lavished upon me. We have a wonderful home. I never tire of looking through the glass into the other greenhouses and comparing to what Zircon has amassed.

The wonder never stopped, because Zircon didn't finish with creations. Ze took time and fiddled with them as ze progressed. Ze created many more things beyond our small apartment. While ze was so engaged, I was enamored of the details in the creations both within and without the space. The pear branch through the one wall was fragrant with blossoms, and a few fruits peppered its length. Somehow all the blossoms were never ripe at one time, and the tree ripened fruit at a rate to feed those who depended on it.

Zircon would often rest in the evenings with me on zir lap. Some nights ze told me stories. "The butterfly has been difficult. I want them to be bigger, smaller, all sizes. But the rules of the world as it has been created only allow them to be so large." Ze pulled one out of nowhere, and the delicate creature opened its gossamer wings. "This is the largest. Over time I think I could get it larger, but the air feels so volatile it might catch fire with the lightning."

I was entranced when the butterfly took flight. Tiny wingbeats propelled it a small distance in any direction, and it didn't simply glide, ever. It perched in the open window, and then disappeared beyond my ken.

"And it's gone. For now. Did you like it?" Ze stared out the window after it, like ze could still experience it even if I could not.

"The butterfly is amazing." I thought about the creatures he had brought, plants and other things. I didn't say my favorite was the mushroom. I knew ze hadn't created them specifically, but ze had modified many of them to fill new purposes.

I didn't tell Zircon. That was my secret, one of a few I wasn't ready to share with zir.

Occasionally I wanted other company, I missed my brethren beyond the apartment, but not enough to tell Zircon of course. Ze and I had fabulous chats about the plants and the tiny animals that peeked through the bushes. Life was almost as perfect as I could imagine.

Until one day Zircon brought home a kitten. The tiny furball played cute, needing more of Zircon's attention than that little slip of a cat ought. Days passed, with all of zir attention on the kitten and nothing left over for me. This was the first time I ever felt alone.

When Zircon was away, the kitten wasn't enough company to alleviate the emptiness. And when ze returned, the kitten had all of his attention. Zircon told the cat that he would be Shadow, and that Shadow had everything he needed here. Shadow was a perfect and moral being, and he should leave the poinsettia on the counter alone.

There might have been a reason for that. I did run amok of that plant when I first got here; my stomach was very upset. The cat could share that vulnerability. Yet Zircon hadn't told me that when I was new. Is that only because I learned the hard way? Something about that warning stuck in my gullet, that Shadow was given warning for something dangerous, and I had to learn on my own. As for being a perfect and moral being, wasn't I all of those things, too? I searched my memories for some kind of answer to that, but more often we spoke about the nature of the things around us, rather than what Zircon and I are.

I kept myself close to Zircon, yet zir love and attention constantly centered on Shadow. I didn't know Shadow from Adam, and I couldn't see much difference to having the cat play in our space. Changes in how Zircon presented zirself to the kitten also became apparent. Ze's attitude was of the creator toward the created. I kept my mouth shut about that point, watching.

The more time I had on my hands to watch, I saw Shadow bow to Zircon. The adoration was so palpable I wanted to choke. I couldn't take the kitten's view of my friend. Ze and I had had a lot of time to know each other on a more level field.

Zircon admonished me to be kinder to the interloper. I acquiesced, as the cat wasn't a bad guy. He even looked to me for support or companionship when ze wasn't around. His tiny nose and whiskers said a lot about him, and the first time I touched his fur, I was amazed by the floof of the being. I didn't see Shadow as Zircon did, but I also knew we weren't on the same level either.

As time passed, Zircon noticed Shadow was lonely and needed a friend. Then ze brought home another cat! This one ze named Angel, and while I could still not really tell the difference between them, their personalities came through soon enough.

I may have been sulking throughout apartment 2B. Shadow and Angel had everything, and they had each other, and why did I still feel apart from all the happenings between them and Zircon? It must have been the accidental contact with the poinsettia. It wasn't my fault, but the experience had changed me.

However, if these favored kittens also touched the poinsettia, I would get my pal back, right? I buried that thought for the right time and place. Since the kittens were my only option, I ended up taking Zircon's advice and I could be caught chilling with them at many points during the day. I learned everything about them and their lives in the apartment paradise.

Shadow was a pretty quiet guy. He often touched Angel, a paw to her paw, brushing himself against her fur, giving her a quiet headbutt to the shoulder, and the very rare nose to nose touch. I interpreted this as affection, and I learned the ways to do it.

Shadow and Angel both appreciated that from me, and I soon joined their bubble of contentment. Angel preferred to keep chatting, telling stories of her discoveries and her joy to learn all that happened through the glass.

Angel's latest discovery was another cat outside the window. "She looked so much like Shadow with those green eyes and fluffy fur, but her whiskers and ears were different shapes."

"I have not seen cats through the window. I haven't found another dragon, either." There was no reason to tell them about the other spirits, my true brethren. We all had our places in the building, and our areas did not overlap. I curled into a ball with the two cats. They decided on naptime, and really there was no reason to break up their routine. Plus naptime with two cats is a very warm and cuddly place to be.

I never skipped naptime. They tended to purr when we all curled into a ball. I thought long and hard about this color nonsense that Angel and Shadow used to tell things apart. Smell worked much better for me, but I needed to learn more.

Naptime didn't last that long. Those cats might sleep a lot, but not for hours at a time. We returned to our idyllic surroundings, and I finally had the idea. "If you two are so interested in all of the things, why don't you study the poinsettia? I know you've learned so much about the other plants in here, and the fruits that come through from the trees. Why not that one?"

"Zircon said no," Shadow said. "Though I do wonder why."

Angel flicked her whiskers. "Ze said we're perfect and moral beings that need nothing else."

"Then why is it here?" Shadow bumped his nose to Angel's. "Do you know, Lucy?"

I knew a lot of things that I didn't exactly share with cats, but that wasn't one of them. All three of us stared at the offending poinsettia that never shared its secrets. "I thought all knowledge was worth having, so I touched it once."

"Would we be different if we touched it?" Shadow rubbed himself against Angel, then me.

Oh, there's no description for the loveliness of his fur against my scales. He's simultaneously warm and cooling as he moves against me. He purred, too, with the rumbling vibration moving over and through my body.

The red blooms of the poinsettia drew us nearer, but Zircon interrupted us. "I have returned!"

Three of us raced toward Zircon as ze closes the door behind zirself. I hung behind while they pounced into his lap. Experience told me I'd get pushed out if I crowded in with them. The cats always received his adoration first, and then I would get acknowledged later. I climbed the chair and rested against the back of Zircon's arm. He grinned at me.

"Such a beautiful day everywhere." Zircon spread his arms. "Do you all love this garden apartment?"

"Of course we do." The call and response of it nagged at me; every day ze shared the news. I'd done it every day before the cats, but it never bothered me when I had all of Zircon's attention. It had only become monotonous as a single question and response since the kittens had arrived. The daily coming together felt like a ritual instead of a shared space.

I found myself tucked inside zir arm, rather than outside. The cats snuggled up against zir torso. I missed when I could have Zircon to myself, to sit in zir lap if I needed. I didn't want to admit how much I wanted that time again, with our long conversations about the world outside and the events that changed it. Since the cats, none of that transpired.

It's not that I wanted them gone, or so I told myself. I just wanted some time like how it had been before. I felt forgotten and overlooked, yesterday's gorgeous leaf crumbling to bits on the counter. Zircon's regard before had been different, and the cats didn't get that from zir, either. Who did ze give that aspect of zirself to? It could be me again, if only the cats weren't so much in the way.

All of this time together with the kittens, and I paid attention to everything. I created a new meat, bacon, with bits from treat-times, and I gently sprinkled tiny pieces from a cabinet above the poinsettia. I didn't want to end up with another stomachache setting a trap for them. I just needed it to be Zircon and me again, at least part of the time. If I put us all on equal footing with the damn poinsettia, I would become the favorite again, though I still didn't know what Zircon's warning meant about the plant.

When I finished, I leapt down to sniff the treat. If I could smell it, surely the kittens would also.

"Why do you love that plant so much?" Angel hopped on the counter behind me.

I hoped she could smell the bacon already. "Why don't you?"

Shadow jumped to the other side of the counter. He sniffed everything. His nose quivered.

I knew he smelled the bacon. He wanted it; he was that kind of cat.

"That plant smells divine." Angel hung at the corner of it. "What could one little touch do?"

Apartment 2B

Shadow and Angel both dipped their heads in the plant, finding the bacon bits, and enjoying the smells.

Zircon found us there. Ze appeared out of nowhere!

All three of us jumped back, guilty.

"You have broken my rule." Ze looked as sad as ze was angry. "You must leave now. Fend for yourselves in the world without my garden apartment."

He picked up both the cats and me, holding us in one arm, and he opened the door and put us outside.

Shadow and Angel huddled on the ground, no doubt the upset stomach caught up with them in this moment. I didn't ask them if the bacon was worth it. I couldn't believe I was tossed out with the rest of the interlopers. As if each of us was easily replaced in Zircon's heart and zir domain.

The cats dragged themselves to the nearest pear branch, in one small bundle of fur.

I'd have joined them, but Zircon caught me by the scruff of my neck. "I know what you did, Lucy." Ze changed me. My form felt stuck, like I was no longer able to switch it at will. My scales remained, though the rest of me felt long and oddly thin. I slithered away, and when the cats saw me they frantically jumped and clung to the branch they had been huddled next to.

Of all the dirty tricks, Zircon has changed me into something they fear. No more catnaps with the bundles of fur and purring. I felt bereft, suddenly, of so much more than just Zircon. Would other beings find me so hideous? What had Ze done to me? I wandered through the buildings to find my own kind, or some other creature who might have mercy for someone of my new shape. The kittens had gotten off easily, and I knew they were still the favorites. I had been completely forsaken, and I would never find my place among them again. Such a cruel move, and if I ever get the chance to repay it, I will.

In the meantime, I discovered catnip. I harvested it as best I could and gave it as a gift to the kittens, now full grown and looking like there would soon be new kittens. When they had the catnip, I again could get the catnaps, no matter what Zircon had done to my body. It was a small consolation in the times that followed. The apartment was no longer accessible, nor could any of us find it again. The world outside couldn't be called a paradise, though it did have the beauty of all the possible things. I couldn't trust others like Zircon, so I steered clear, hoping only to find my brethren as they, too, ran amok of the creators.

Ransom Noble writes speculative fiction stories. They're fascinated by creatures, mythological and alien and technological and everything in between. They reside near Madison, Wisconsin with their family until the call of adventure leads them to new places and ideas. Find out more at ransomnoble.com.

Lussinaten

Catherine Schaff-Stump

The floor was covered with rushes. Dogs snuffled among the dried grass, looking for food; bolder ones climbed the table. Most of the house was asleep, but Quartz kept her vigil by the fireplace, soaking in what little heat Alfheim afforded. Tonight had been a night for pretending to be the king's lover, but she was tired of playing that role. Then again, when wasn't she playing a role?

King Feldspar, pale as a December lake, whispered loud enough to be heard over the sleep breathing of mortal men, the snoring, and the mumbling. The great fire crackled and snapped as Quartz leaned closer, turning her ear toward his lips, so close his breath tickled her ear.

"We have an understanding?" His hand reached out to touch her leg.

"We do," she said. Quartz took his hand, cold as ice, and held it. His breath smelled of aquavit, anise seed mixing with the perfume of smoke. "You leave tonight, and you will bring her back."

Tonight, because it was Lussinaten, when the veils between Alfheim and Midgard were thinnest. Quartz stood. The metal caps on the end of her dark braids grazed the carved bench where she had sat, one tracing an angular rune. The fire cast her shadow stuttering across the uneven stone floor, rushes rustling underfoot. Quartz watched Feldspar study the flickering shadows, his eyes empty tunnels, and Quartz wondered if it were true what the Christians said about the elves, that their kind had no souls.

Feldspar spoke again. "Bring her back. You can kill him."

Quartz grabbed a fur from the pile by the door. It smelled earthy. Outside the hall, raindrops spat from a starless sky. Quartz cupped her palm and caught a few. The drops froze in her hand.

She had permission to kill him. Quartz turned her hand over and the frozen crystals spilled to the ground. It was as close to tears as she could ever get.

§

"Well?" said Quartz. One braid swung over her shoulder as she turned toward laughter, scraping from a crag of rock on the ground. "What is it that amuses you, troll?"

The rock unfolded itself. Barrel-like arms ground and crunched away from the boulder's center. A tremor stuttered the ground as the troll stretched itself in the twilight. Mossy hair dangled over a carved face, rectangular jaw, bulbous nose. It blinked piggy eyes at the last vestiges of the sun sinking under the horizon and brushed snow off its shoulders.

"You stepped from the branches of Yggdrasil, didn't you?" The troll scratched its side and pebbles rained on the ground.

Quartz waved away rock dust from her face. "What nonsense are you spouting?"

"How long has it been since you crossed into Midgard?" the troll repeated.

Quartz thought stone creatures patient and slow. "Not so long," she said.

The troll's jaw crackled. "What brings you here? Lussinaten?"

Quartz sighed. She was wasting a lot of words on this nosey troll. "Why should I explain myself to you?"

"No reason. Your people and mine, we've never seen eye to eye." It rumbled, its shoulders shaking, more pebbles pinging off the rocks. It spared her the obvious joke, something like, because you're too short.

Quartz tapped her foot, pebbles aggravating her sole under her soft leather shoes. "You want to know why I'm here?"

The troll looked away. "Not that it's any of my business."

Quartz tilted her head back, looking up at the piggy eyes. "It is not. You should know your better and act accordingly."

The troll scoffed. "Now, there's an attitude that will get you into trouble."

"I only speak truth."

The troll's shoulders heaved, and again there was the sound of scraping. "You elves have no idea how things are changing. The villages near here are full of Norwegian farmers. If you ask them, they will tell you they have no betters." The troll slammed its fist into a hand. "They even beat their own priests."

"Is that so?" Quartz had heard the old religions were being challenged. "Have the farmers decided to chase the Christians out?"

"Quite the reverse," said the troll. "There are laws against beating priests. They will do it anyway, the ornery ones. Wouldn't we all like to beat a priest?"

Quartz rubbed her shoulders. "Why don't you, a great brute like you?"

"Now it's you who's making fun of me," said the troll. The troll lifted a foot and thought about putting it down. Trolls moved in their own time. "Take my advice. With the right clothes, you can pass for a mortal. It's Lussinaten. They expect that sort of thing, gods, and elves, and what not. And why not?"

"Have you seen others of my kind?" Quartz asked.

"In the village." The troll's leg pummeled the ground. Once that column was in place, it lifted the other. "Follow the sleigh tracks. You can't miss them."

§

Since there was no cross above the door to keep her out, Quartz climbed the cold wooden steps into the barn. On the way, she'd modified her seeming to fit into this more modern Midgard. She tucked wayward brown hair under a bonnet. The embroidered *bunad* she wore over her blouse was the same pattern as that of the dancing mortals twirling on the floor. She could pass for one of them with her dark hair and eyes if they didn't look too closely. Even if they did, the troll was right. Tonight was one of the few nights they wouldn't care.

Warm air and fresh grain from the loft mixed with the smell of spiced apples and lingonberries. The homey smell of horse was barely covered by the food. She blended into a group of young women by the wooden bowl of sweet soup. Red-hatted *nisse*, feet dangling from the rafters, bobbed their heads to a *hardanger* reel. One of them winked at her. She took a bowl of sweet soup, which cooled in her hands. Lanterns hung from nails in the walls, fending off the longest night.

A young man, breathless from the dance floor, came up to her. He was broad and sturdy, the way a mortal would be after a life of plowing the land or casting nets. "Would you like to dance?"

"No." Quartz drank the soup before all the warmth leached away, letting the spices run over her tongue, tints and textures of cinnamon and cloves, the only heat the winter elves of Alfheim would ever know. What would drinking something hot be like?

"Oh, come on!"

Quartz blinked. "We haven't even been introduced properly."

The mortal waved his hand across his face, a movement of dismissal. "No one cares for that sort of thing anymore. If you insist, I'm Daniel." He stuck out his hand. "You'll regret it if you come to a Lussinaten party, and you don't dance. Maybe not today, but later. Perhaps for the rest of your life."

The rest of her life was likely to be some time. "I can't." She felt herself cooling with embarrassment. "I've never done it."

"You'll see. It's dead easy."

Quartz placed the wooden bowl on a shelf behind her where it was whisked away by one of the tiny *nisse* before a mortal could catch a glimpse of his red hat. The opening doors fanned in gusts of cold air.

Quartz gave Daniel her hands and he trotted backwards onto the dance floor. Swirling couples circled around them.

"Cross hands," Daniel said over the fiddle. "My left to your left." She grabbed both of his calloused hands. "That's right. Now, we swing."

Quartz was not used to swinging. She leaned away from the center, and her weight stretched their arms, made her feel like she was tumbling and running, all at the same time. She laughed.

Daniel laughed. "Give me your elbow," he shouted.

Quartz stopped and studied her elbow.

"No!" He hooked his arm though hers and they were spinning again. Flying, without leaving the ground. What it might be like for Janetta in the storm, out of control. Quartz mustn't forget she was here on a mission, looking for Janetta and looking for him.

The room spiraled, and her heart fluttered. All she thought about was the movement of her feet as she spun. Not about kings and winter and other things. It was a moment inside of herself, for herself. The gift of a stranger to her.

The music stopped. "Thank you," Quartz said. "I will never forget this."

Daniel laughed. "So serious. Would you like to go flying?"

"I don't fly," she said.

"Suit yourself." Daniel left her, running to another young woman who knew him, who peeled herself away from the wall. They joined another couple.

The mortals danced with abandon like *hulders*. Two men supported two women who lifted their feet from the floor. The women flew in the air drifting like clouds over the mountains.

Quartz stared at them. Skirts fluttered and the women bobbed. She caught glimpses of lace petticoats. Lantern lights glinted off the silver buckles of the men's shoes.

So that was flying. She might want that after all.

Quartz steadied herself, ignored the music, and focused on what came next. The other couple dancing with Daniel and his partner were Janetta, the Winter Queen, and Siegfried, her kinsman and co-conspirator.

The Winter Queen's bonnet tumbled from her head as she twirled. Her pale hair fanned out like a blanket of snow, a moment where what Janetta actually was and what Janetta pretended to be blurred. The dancers slowed, and Siegfried lowered Janetta to the barn's floor. The cold glow of pleasure in Janetta's cheeks made Quartz want to dance even more.

The fiddle stopped with a flourish, and Daniel's partner woman ran back to the sidelines. Siegfried, tall and muscular, overshadowed Janetta. Did Daniel notice that Janetta was unnaturally cold when he put his hand on her shoulder, or did her blouse cushion him from that?

More partners positioned themselves on the floor. Quartz clasped her hands together and took a deep breath. Time to get this over with. She weaved among the small circles of dancers toward Daniel, Siegfried, and Janetta, who was enjoying something Daniel said.

Janetta saw Quartz and her laughter died. Siegfried stepped in front of Janetta, a move that did not go unnoticed by Daniel.

"You danced well," Quartz said. "Where did you learn the mortal dances?"

"Why are you here?" Siegfried asked. Never time for pleasantries, Siegfried.

Daniel cleared his throat. "Now. Everyone has the right to come to the party. Especially tonight."

"Not her," Siegfried said.

The dancers moved with the precision of a clock around them, the inner circle moving to new partners in the outer circle. The new couples grasped hands and swung.

"Thank you, Daniel," Quartz said over the music. "Your kindness is something others could learn."

Janetta stepped between Quartz and Siegfried. "We can't talk here," Janetta said.

"I don't want you going anywhere with her," said Siegfried.

"All of us," said Janetta. "We'll all go."

Quartz shook her head. "Daniel, stay here." Their business did not concern him, mortal that he was. He could get hurt, and if Feldspar took a hand, possibly worse.

"No. Come with us," said Janetta. "I will feel safer."

Siegfried scowled. He had shaved his beard, so he could blend in, drawing attention to mountain blue eyes and a strong chin. No, Quartz reminded herself. She wanted to kill him.

Why would Janetta assume a mortal would make her safer?

Outside the barn, the snowflakes floated like puffs of escaped wool. Daniel huddled in his coat. "I don't know how you stay warm without a coat, on a night like this."

"Guess." Quartz moved closer to Janetta. Siegfried moved closer to Quartz. The scent of food lingered on Daniel's coat. Roasted elk.

"I know you are from Alfheim," said Daniel. "I am amazed at how you don't feel the cold."

The music and laughter echoed from tree to tree. Some of the revelers hitched horses to wagons. Torches lit their way in the dark night, twinkling like grounded stars.

Quartz tilted her head and studied Daniel. Was there something about him she wasn't seeing? "How would you know that I am from Alfheim?"

"Janetta has claimed sanctuary with me," said Daniel. "You must be someone who has been sent for her."

Quartz had not suspected that Janetta would be so clever. "You…are a holy man?"

Daniel looked down at his feet and blushed. "Not as holy as some."

"But you are a priest?" Quartz was confused. "If you know what we are, you know we are...unloved by your God." Thus, Janetta should not have found sanctuary.

"Not my God," said Daniel. "Anyone is allowed to seek sanctuary with the church."

No. That didn't make sense at all. "Has she been in the church?"

"I have been hiding her in my home."

For all the Winter Queen's beauty, she looked like a smug ermine. Quartz wanted to slap her. "Your husband wants you to come home. You have responsibilities."

"No," said Janetta. "You do it. You want to."

What nonsense was this? "You know that's not possible. I am not you. I am not the storm." Even if Quartz had the ability, she would not, for all the magic in Alfheim, attach herself so to Feldspar.

"Why not? You take my place in his bed."

Quartz slapped Janetta. Siegfried's hand shot around Quartz's wrist.

"Try that again, and I will rip your hand off." Siegfried tightened his grip.

Janetta's cheek showed the beginning of a bruise. "I won't forget this."

Quartz gasped. The small bones in her wrist popped. What was it the trolls said? Grind their bones to make my bread. "Come back," Quartz said through her teeth. "Please."

Janetta placed her hands behind her back and rocked on her feet like a small girl. "Siegfried, please dispose of her."

Siegfried nodded curtly. "Neither of you need to see this."

"Don't do anything you will regret," Daniel said. He led Janetta toward a wagon.

"If she wanted to keep other women out of Feldspar's bed, she should give him a reason to stay in hers," Quartz muttered.

Siegfried twisted her arm behind her, and Quartz hissed. She walked in front of him on tiptoe, and he pushed her into the tiny sauna building of the farm.

"Sit!" Siegfried forced Quartz onto the bench. The building smelled of birch and juniper. Quartz contemplated taking one of the dry stones from the center basin and braining him with it. Instead, she rubbed the ache in her shoulder.

"What will you do now? Kill me?" If their positions were reversed, it's what she would have done.

Siegfried was close to her, so close. The tiny room was full of him. "Why did you come?"

"You know why."

"She doesn't want to go back. You know how he uses her."

"He uses everyone. If she weren't so stupid, she could manage him. She holds all the power. She makes the winter."

"You betrayed her," said Siegfried. "You chose Feldspar."

Quartz stood. Their bodies were inches apart. There was the smell of old wood, the memory of steam between them. "She tells you to jump off the Sognefjord and you'd do it!"

"I support my cousin!"

"You defied your king!"

"You slept with Feldspar!"

"Yes!" Quartz hammered his chest with her fists. "You stupid man! I slept with him! He listens to me now! And I could have made something of you!"

"I want nothing to do with you! You faithless— "

"Me? You unforgiving, myopic— "

Quartz cut off her own words. In the haze of her anger, she covered his mouth with her own. Siegfried's arms pulled her in, and they tumbled to sitting half the bench, half on the floor. Siegfried tangled her dark hair in his thick fingers, pulling her head back. His lips and tongue foraged, finding her neck.

Quartz peeled back his jacket and silver buttons popped, ricocheting off the basin holding the stones. She ripped his shirt away and raked her nails across the cold skin of his chest, her fingers tracing frost ripples on his skin.

"Rough," Siegfried muttered. "That's new."

Quartz bit his ear.

Siegfried lifted her up, hitching her skirt. She wrapped her legs around his waist. They leaned against the wall and the building trembled. He fumbled with the buttons of his trousers.

Janetta's voice called for him from outside, like a pathetic child.

They stood still for a moment, both of them on the precipice of lust.

"I have to go," said Siegfried. His hands opened the neck of her shirt, and his mouth was kissing the tops of her breasts.

"Stay," said Quartz. Her lips grazed over his cheeks, his beard stubble scratching her lips. She had been empty without him. Quartz kissed every part of him that she could reach. "Don't go."

Siegfried lowered her, gently. The scratches on his chest were inky scars against his pale skin. "I promised her. "

"She will always be more important than me." Quartz's skirt swirled around her legs. "I understand."

"She is family. I am honor bound."

"I understand. Honor is more important than me." Quartz tied the neck of her shirt closed. The ghost of his hungry kisses still electrified her skin.

"This was a mistake," said Siegfried.

Quartz clenched her fists. Her knuckles turned white. Her voice was flat. "Yes. You're right. That felt wrong. Like a mistake. Exactly."

"What do you want me to do?" The way he looked at her, wanting her, but not allowing himself.

Men. They were so weak. "Let me take her home," said Quartz. "If I don't bring her back, Feldspar will come."

"Let him." Siegfried picked up his jacket.

"Let him?" Quartz followed Siegfried. "He will kill you because you are a traitor. Do you want to die?"

Siegfried had finished dressing, as much as he could. "If I must." He stumbled, hit one of the benches, and picked himself up. Again, he stumbled. His hand went to his head. He stared at her. He knew. He missed reaching for her, and he fell again. This time, he stayed on the hard, cold floor.

"Inevitable," Quartz whispered, crouching. "You are dying for something foolish."

"What have you done?" Siegfried's voice was so quiet, so weak.

Her lips caressed his forehead. She closed his fluttering eyes. "I kissed you," she said. "And I poisoned you."

§

The snow grew vicious. The wind plucked away Quartz's bonnet and tangled her hair into a wild bird's nest. Pebbles of sleet stung her face. Her clothes stiffened with ice. She was grateful for the troll, both as a guide and as partial shelter.

"There." The gangly arm of the troll pointed at the church. The wagon ruts had only gone so far before the snow covered them, but the troll knew where it was. All churches were brown on the outside, a cross between a Viking ship and a gingerbread house. Points pyramided on each other as the church climbed heavenward toward the Christian god, whom she had yet to see. But Quartz's kind heard him in church bells and felt him in the Christian symbols. Behind the church was the outline of a small house, made hazy by the storm.

"Tried breaking in there once," said the troll. "Felt like I'd been struck by lightning."

"Could it be any worse than this?" Quartz could barely hear the troll's deep voice against the wind.

"Yes," said the troll. "May the gods grant you victory."

"I won't forget I owe you a favor."

The snow gathered in the crags and recesses of his body. "I won't forget either."

Quartz slid down the hill, barking her shins on the icy rocks. She fought with wild tangles of her hair, pulling the strands away from her face. The trees whipped. Branches tumbled across the ground not far away.

A whirlwind of ice beads blew up around her, slicing her skin. Then the veil of storm cleared, hovering. Above her, riding the north wind, Janetta, the Winter Queen, revealed herself. Thoughts crystallized in Quartz's mind. Siegfried wasn't protecting Janetta. He stabilized her, and now he was gone.

"Where is my cousin?" Janetta shouted. "Where is Siegfried?"

"Stop this," said Quartz. "This storm will kill all in its path."

"I. Will. Not. Go. Back!" A veil of ice and snow solidified and sliced the air, a blade of execution intending to scrape Quartz's offense from the earth.

Quartz ran past the church. There was no sanctuary for her there. She struggled against the wind, climbing steps to the door of the small house. A cross hung above the door, and Quartz couldn't knock. Janetta's deadly ice glinted in the gold torchlight of the windows.

"Priest!" Quartz yelled. "Open the door."

Janetta's ice sheet struck the wall, gouging the wood. A splinter scraped Quartz's skin. She fell to her knees and felt the ice blade shave strands of her hair. It arced behind her and came again for another slice.

The door opened and Daniel pulled her inside. Quartz's ears rustled with the sounds of angry whispers from Christian angels. The priest slammed the door as the ice hit it. The wall rattled and the wind howled.

Daniel moved his lips, but she couldn't hear what he said. The whispering faded and became a ringing. "Do you still think," Quartz said, "that she needs protecting?"

Daniel clutched a Bible with both hands. "What is wrong with her?"

"She is a force of nature. She doesn't care about any of us." Yes, that was right.

Daniel shook. Whether it was from worry or touching her, Quartz couldn't be certain. "That's not the Janetta I know. Where is Siegfried?"

"We're on our own." Quartz pulled herself from the floor. "She likes you. Do you think you could calm her?"

The pane in the single glass window shattered. Daniel shielded Quartz and the fragments spilled onto his shirt. "Can't you...magic her or something?"

"That's not the kind of magic I do." The roof creaked and peeled away with a roar, waving like a leaf caught in the wind. Daub and dust rained down on them.

"Run for the church," Daniel said.

"I can't go in the church."

Daniel grabbed her arm and pulled her. "You must. You won't enjoy it much, but I'll get you through it."

They ran, the walls of the house falling around them. One of them took to the air. A flying wheel hit Daniel in the chest. Quartz knew Daniel was right. Neither of them would survive out here in Janetta's temper tantrum.

They pushed into the church, the two of them forcing the doors open against the storm, barely squeezing through. The church voices slapped her and drowned out all other sound. The pressure in her chest felt like she was being squeezed between two millstones. Quartz fell to her knees in front of the cross at the altar. Glowing energy threaded through her skin with needles of light. She screamed.

Wind blasted through the oak doors, blowing them inward. Heretic! Blasphemer! Quartz covered her ears and lurched toward Daniel.

The troll had been right. This was torment. Quartz would take her chances in the storm. Pushing past Daniel, she stumbled into the snow. When Quartz's head stopped echoing, she saw Janetta lying on the ground, glowing white as her storm magic cooled. Lussinaten was ending, and Janetta was running out of magic.

Quartz's temple was sticky, liquid, cold and thick. She was bleeding. Daniel came out of the church. He pointed to a cloud overhead, angry, and bulbous, full of lightning inside and out. He said something about it, but Quartz could hear only the howl of the wind.

Feldspar rode down from the cloud, his shaggy ponies kicking up mist. With him was Siegfried, leading the second, riderless horse. He would not meet Quartz's eyes.

Words were becoming clearer if she focused on them, but she couldn't understand exactly what Siegfried was saying to Feldspar. "…was never…she…madness."

Quartz moved toward Feldspar. She knew her voice would be too loud. "You didn't need to come."

"I trusted you to kill Siegfried." Feldspar surveyed the wreckage of the house. The church stood tall, unscratched. "You failed me."

"I thought I would kill him," said Quartz. When it came down to it, one did not kill what one loved, but Quartz could hardly explain that to Feldspar. "She needs her cousin, for balance. You need both of them."

"Take care of her," Feldspar ordered Siegfried.

"You don't have to obey him," said Daniel. He stepped forward, but Quartz raised her hand to stop him moving forward.

"You're not inside your god's house," said Quartz. "Choose your actions carefully.

Siegfried picked Janetta up, her hair dangling, pieces of it flaking into ice, some of it melting. He laid her carefully on the riderless pony. "There's nothing more for you here, Daniel. She tried to leave, and she failed. I am honor bound to take care of her wherever she is."

"She said she didn't want to go. You can't take her like this." Daniel struck down Quartz's arm and walked forward.

Siegfried shook his head. "It's no longer your concern, Daniel. "

"I can't let you. She sought sanctuary. I am charged by God to stop you."

Feldspar patted the horse behind him. "Come, Quartz."

Quartz grabbed Daniel's arm. "You've seen what she's done. You know she can't stay here. None of us can or should."

Daniel shook Quartz off and marched forward.

Feldspar raised a hand. Icicles shot up from the ground and spiked through him. "Enough of this," said Feldspar. He had dismissed Daniel just like he would a bone picked clean of meat.

Quartz and Siegfried reached Daniel at the same time. Daniel's breathing was labored. Blood tinted the icicles pink. "Break them off," said Quartz, "carefully."

Siegfried cracked the icicles, his jaw set. He said nothing.

A tremor ran through Daniel's body as Daniel slid into the frozen snow. "So cold," he said.

Quartz knelt. She put a finger to his lips.

"There's nothing more we can do," said Siegfried. "You have to come now."

"No." Quartz grabbed his hand. "He will die."

"Come now," said Siegfried.

She was tired, weary. She was tired of using others, and of being used. "You have your duty," said Quartz. "I am taking a different path."

Siegfried stared at her. He could never imagine life without service, even if the service was to the mad rulers of Alfheim. He could never understand. Revolution was hard, especially for their kind.

"Women are weak," said Feldspar. "Even this one. I thought I had trained you to be a vicious dog. You defy me, Quartz?"

"My lord," said Quartz, with a nod of her head, "I cannot come with you."

"Well, then." Feldspar raised a hand. "You will never see our land again." His smile was cruel. "All you have ever wanted is power," said Feldspar. "Now you will have nothing."

Quartz knelt by Daniel until the hoof beats disappeared, kneeling in the snow as the sun climbed into the sky.

Quartz watched Daniel's chest rise and fall. She held his hand and used her dirty apron to bind wounds and staunch blood. She wasn't sure what to do next. If she left him, he might die. If she moved him, he might die. If they could make it to the church, she would die.

Warm tears streaked her face. Warm tears. Her fingers touched warm tears.

She shivered in the cold. All of her was freezing, except for the fire inside of her, the ember of her new soul.

Cath Schaff-Stump writes fantasy for children and adults. She writes funny stories, dark stories, and everything in between. She is the author of the Klaereon Scroll series and the Abigail Rath Versus series. More of her fiction has been published by Paper Golem Press, Daydreams Dandelion Press, and in *The Mammoth Book of Dieselpunk*. You can find her online at Facebook, Goodreads, Amazon, @cathschaffstump, and cathschaffstump.com. Follow Cath's Kindle Vella serial *The Autumn Warrior and the Ice Sword*. Catherine was a finalist in the 2022 Next Generation Indie Awards for Horror fiction.

THE CHIMERA'S QUIET REVOLT

ATHENA FOSTER

Charlie had zero interest in fairy politics, and less-than-zero interest in fairy *family* politics, but he needed to engage in both if he was going to attend the Dream Actors Guild awards. While he was waiting for Luca to arrive for their "emergency" meeting, Charlie kept busy doing some edits on the latest episode for his channel. His studio fit into the second bedroom of his apartment, which was easy to do since all he needed was a bed with a DreamRec helmet and large display and interface to do the finishing. He couldn't tell anyone at the Guild that he was legally dead and only lived again due to the Halfling trick of a secret fairy House. That would be a trip to HR.

At the moment, House Shelley's reanimated corpses all resided in very *efficient* enclaves buried beneath acre-large solar rectifiers. Great source of energy for re-animations but dangerous for people that objected to getting clipped by a stray microwave. Charlie's AI had said that Luca was on his way in, but Luca had to take the long way since his Quarterling flesh cooked just as well as a regular human. Elena would bake too if she were careless, but as the Halfling of the House that whole spontaneously-return-from-death stunt kept her bases covered. Everyone else that lived here didn't care so much.

A quiet knock and Charlie left his desk to open the door. Luca came in quickly, and Charlie shut the door with due haste. A conversation in the hall would throw off the timing of everything. Luca, a nice young man in his forties who looked more like a movie star than a microbiologist, had the Italian features that his mother Elena lacked, despite being born in Italy. His father had been an Italian fashion model which reinforced the well-known fact that Elena was weak to a pretty face. He collapsed onto the bed, covering his eyes with his forearm, and asked, "Why did you ask me to come in person instead of a video call?"

Charlie had a dozen reasons, but he replied as he returned to his desk, "Because your mother's AI is overprotective, and we're probably going to give her a panic attack today."

Luca raised his arm to look at Charlie, clearly aghast, and said, "Pretend like I've been paying attention to an experiment *every* two hours for the past week and have been sleeping in one-hour increments."

Despite the fact that Luca now looked older than Charlie, who would forever be a twenty-six-year-old black man, Charlie remembered when Luca was a child and had needed obvious advice. So he said, "That isn't sustainable, Luca. Get your lab tech to do it while you sleep."

"I...of course, Charlie. That's a great idea." Which confirmed that the experiment must be related to Luca's trick. Every Halfling House had a primary House trick (Elena could reanimate the dead). But the Quarterlings, having less faerie traits to express, might or might not have a trick, and it might or might not be the same as their Halfling parent. Charlie knew that Luca was working with other Quarterlings from other houses that were willing to work with a House that wasn't out. Now Charlie knew for sure that Luca was working with his own trick.

Charlie didn't press it though. "So to elucidate, your mother sometimes gets panic attacks when we talk about bringing the House out, and her AI has stopped letting us schedule with her if it catches wind of the agenda."

"But you think it will treat me better because I'm a Quarterling and not a chimera?" Luca seemed skeptical.

"No, but it's not supposed to cancel your scheduled time with your mother without her permission or *interrupt* when you two are together. And as long as we stay on the DL, we can go into her lab before the AI catches us and break the news without being stopped.

"We're prepping here in the studio because my recording set-up has to be able to detect other live microphones for copyright and feedback reasons. My work AI will notify me when or if your mother's AI starts listening, so I know it's safe to talk right now. I figured you'd get me in the door to break the news."

Luca's brow furrowed. "Don't you mean talk her into it?"

This was the first time tonight that Charlie would tell a fairy that House Shelley's chimera were in quiet revolt. The last chimera to make a jailbreak from the enclaves had finally made it to her destination at the lunar colony. Everyone else had made a clean getaway over a week ago, but he couldn't blame her for having so much farther to go. The wait had been a mixture of dread and impatience.

Charlie thought Luca could handle it straight, so he jumped right in. "House Shelley has definitely soft launched into the world. After the courts decided House LeMoine vs Brood K-2050 and the plastic eating caterpillars were allowed to both join a Waste Management Union and *leave* their House while still retaining their faerie legal status, the other chimera weren't willing to wait for Elena."

Luca's face transitioned from confused to still, except for his eyes tracking back and forth as he processed. He sat up and perched on the edge of the bed. Charlie could smell some cortisol rolling off him. Might as well lay it all out before he started asking questions.

Charlie dove back in, "We know she thinks keeping the chimera in the enclaves and keeping House Shelly hidden is for everyone's safety. But those kids, re-animated by converted sunlight with their ethically sourced corpses, they really feel like all their chimeric modifications are superhero powers to go fight climate change. Everyone that wanted to go is now out in the world trying to test all their modifications in real settings, especially the poly-extremophiles. Those folks couldn't wait to get out there." Charlie threw his hands in the air like it was out of his control, even though he'd agreed with all their decisions and continued, "I wish I could say that I was going to do the same, but I just want to go to the DAG awards."

Luca perked up, "Did you get nominated again?"

Charlie nodded. "Best Period Piece. Little do they know that if you were animated in the 1940s, you can dream like it's the 1940s."

"If you go, they might find out you're cheating." Luca sounded wistful. He knew what would happen when Charlie went out in public. FaceID would ID him; he was out of the statute of limitations on image privacy protections.

"It's not cheating." Charlie retorted,"I still recorded a real dream and didn't do anything but let the Guild's AI fill in bits that failed to render from the recorder. Same as anyone else." Charlie didn't mention that the Guild was putting pressure on him to attend and take a meeting with an unnamed House regarding his dreams.

Luca slapped both his knees, like an old man, "Fine. Everyone is coming out. House Shelley is out, as soon as someone notices. Why do you need me for this?"

"I want to break it to Elena without giving her a full-on panic attack. She's still your mom and likes to keep her shit together in front of you. Just because we've taken up our agency doesn't mean we can't do our best to be kind about it."

§

Charlie and Luca stood together in the windowless hallway outside Elena's lab. Bright white light shone from wall sconces and opera leaked out from underneath the door.

Luca tugged at the sleeves of his lab coat, which he only wore when he wanted to remind his mother of his doctorates.

"Are you going to knock?" Charlie asked.

"I don't normally knock." Luca replied, sounding defensive.

"Then quit your dilly-dallying if you want to get back to your lab." Charlie might have been less harsh if he was less nervous.

The Chimera's Quiet Revolt

Luca opened the door and sidled into the lab. Charlie paused in the doorway as he was assaulted by ear-shattering remixed Italian opera. It must be an infusion day.

Elena crouched in the center of the room next to her re-sus tank, which was a cross between a mortician's slab and an aquarium. Her fingers were deftly connecting a hanging bag of fluid to a small pump. Her dark hair had been piled haphazardly over her narrow face, which bore a look too weary for someone who appeared to be in their late twenties.

A fresh corpse lay submerged in gel, except for the head, which was wedged up above the surface. The gel maintained the body at a stable temperature while the pump moved various solutions through the body's circulatory system. The sound of thunder came in like a notification sound on top of the opera track. Elena said it helped with the fairy magic; Charlie was skeptical.

She stood up and smiled warmly at Charlie, but her eyes narrowed when she turned her gaze to Luca. She waved her hand repeatedly over a nearby sensor and the volume of the music receded to tolerable levels. Then she asked, "What brings you two into the lab today?" And without waiting for a reply she added, "Luca, would you hang a bag of *Thermococcus gammatolerans*? About half a liter should do, I think."

Luca zipped back into stores, abandoning Charlie with evident glee. Now put upon to stall, Charlie could only remember what he'd planned to say. "Elena, I have some news to report. The chimera got together and decided it was time for some of us to leave the enclaves."

She briefly stopped injecting and stared at him blank faced before she continued the injection, though her hands were shaking now. She said, "What do you mean? I haven't found my Method."

Charlie sighed. She must have known it would come to this one day. Halflings usually had a very complicated trick often with extra facets. One would think re-animating corpses would be enough for one person, but Elena could also chimerize her re-animated corpses with bacterial and viral factors. Her work was so genius it was still only possible with fairy magic, but the unbreakable truth of fairy tricks was that they were ultimately possible with normal science.

Some Houses had been able to develop a Method where normal (human) scientists could reproduce their trick without a fairy present. Elena always said the House shouldn't go public until she found her Method.

Charlie responded after a pause, "It's not a catastrophe. We're not all leaving, just those of us that want to do stuff out in the world."

Luca came back into the room and started hanging the bag on one of the other arms of the stand his mother was using.

She jerked around to face him, asking, "Did you know about this?"

"I found out today, but I think that House Shelley going public is a good thing." He replied, speaking softly.

She turned back to Charlie, "*You're* still here. Did anyone else...recognizable...go out?"

Charlie knew she was asking if anyone currently upcycling a famous corpse had gone out. He replied, "Jennifer went out, but she looks different enough that FaceID shouldn't spot her."

Elena huffed. "That girl. Where did she go?" Her hands had stopped shaking.

Charlie fetched a stool from the counter against the wall and sat before he responded, "Marianas Trench, I think. Or maybe she was Chernobyl?" He shrugged.

Elena finished with the settings on the pump and moved over to her workbench to plop into an office chair. "We can't come out until I find the Method. I have to be able to do the modifications to living creatures, not just corpses. People will feel threatened if only dead people are safe from radiation or can breathe water. They'll feel like I'm trying to replace them and they'll come for us. I've seen it before. Besides, we're all so weird."

As a former corpse, Charlie felt like Elena did not appreciate the weirdness of the internet and the changes in society in the past half century. Sometimes she acted like an acclaimed microbiologist, and sometimes she acted like a nineteenth century orphan Halfling, the product of Faerie and the genius of Mary Shelley.

Of course she was both, but Elena's propensity for animating the dead even as a toddler caused the Shelleys to reject her and even officially declare her dead. Even though family friends took her in, she still assumed people would reject her.

Charlie looked to Luca to jump in, but Luca adamantly shook his head no. Charlie scowled. What good was calling backup who wouldn't back you up? He continued, "What do you want to do, Elena? You could stay in hiding. Disown your chimera. Reject them and try to pressure the rest of us to stay in hiding. Unless House Shelley comes out, they won't have protective status, including the exemptions from…anything. Being dead, not having a government identity, needing to be assessed by the FDA, quarantine as a potential biological hazard. We made a list somewhere, but I didn't memorize it."

"I wish they'd stayed." She drummed her fingers on the counter, brow drawn together.

Luca had finished hanging the infusion, but he lingered by the gel bed. He added, "You know that other fairy creations have actually collectivized and House LeMoine's plastic eating caterpillar brood petitioned to join their Waste Management Union and the union reps negotiated their *independence* from House LeMoine."

"Charlie here is planning to go to the Dream Actors Guild Awards, because he's been nominated again. Everyone thinks he'll win this year, and he's never been able to go and celebrate with his friends." Luca clearly refrained from voicing accusatory tones, but expressions of guilt passed over Elena's face in waves. She collapsed back into her chair with her hands limp in her lap. Charlie appreciated the vote of confidence but felt like Luca was laying it on too thick.

Luca continued, "The Dream Actor's Guild is really active. They're always looking out for their members. They're transnational and have no problem working with a person with no official identity, but their turnover means we keep getting new people concerned about Charlie. I keep having to defuse wellness checks, because his liaison keeps thinking he's being falsely imprisoned or blackmailed or something." Charlie wasn't sure if Luca was making that up or if that had actually happened.

Charlie could smell changes in Elena's pheromones which in his experience were associated with fight-or-flight activation. Usually this presaged either a panic attack or a guilt spiral, neither of which was what they were after. So he drew his chair closer and took her hands in his. "Elena, have you been breathing? Living things need to breathe. You're not under attack; you're safe. No one is coming here. No one knows where you are. It's just us: your friend Charlie and your son Luca. We are here to help and support you." The simulated lightning strikes over the music had been escalating, which couldn't be helping the situation, though he knew she had a complicated relationship with lightning.

Elena closed her eyes and started her breathing routine, which was what Charlie had wanted. She gripped his hands tightly before he could disengage, as she did sometimes. He often wondered if the reassurance he was providing was physical contact or his physical appearance. The fact that she closed her eyes just muddled the question further. They were real panic attacks though, so ultimately it didn't *really* matter.

Charlie noticed that Luca was throwing some very expectant glances at his mother as the thunder intensity continued to increase, but she was deep in her meditation and had seemingly blocked everything out. Luca rolled his eyes dramatically and then moved to the end of the tank by the corpse's head.

The thunder from the track had crescendoed into a constant barrage of boom after boom. He gave one last look at his mother before placing his hand on the forehead of the corpse and flipping the large switch at the head of the tank. The lights flickered, though Charlie knew that was part of the process and not due to lack of power. The room hummed with power, electricity coursing through the corpse, causing the limbs to seize and shake, though the gel muted the effect.

Charlie could feel waves of magnetization coming off the tank and instinctually moved to put himself between the tank and Elena, before remembering that normally she was the one standing right next to the tank. He thought he would be fine since he knew he had a fair bit of magnetic reluctance, but he felt strange and dynamic in a way he normally didn't. The feeling kept getting bigger and bigger, and he began breathing fast up in his chest. There was a sudden awareness of all the different foreign prokaryotic colonies chimerized in his body, and it felt like they were changing. He suddenly believed that they had an agenda, and they were, at least in that moment, aware of him as the environment they inhabited and had adapted for their own use.

Elena's eyes popped open, and her jaw dropped as she turned her startled gaze to the tank and her son. Luca, who had been watching her the whole time, had a wry smile on his face. Charlie hadn't expected him to reveal any of *his* secrets today.

Elena said, "Luca, you can create chimera?" She sounded hurt. Charlie had figured out that Luca had a trick, but not that it was the same as Elena's.

Luca flipped the switch off and just like that, Charlie felt dull but still buzzy. He no longer had any sense of a burgeoning revolution going on inside his body.

Luca responded, "I can, but I generally prefer not to reanimate human remains. It's caused you a lot of angst, so I decided to learn from that and avoid it in my own life. I do have a bunch of mice, though. I may have been sneaking them out of your labs in my pockets since I was young."

Elena looked nonplussed. "I thought you couldn't. You didn't tell me."

Luca winced, "I just wanted to do my own research. Do it my own way. Not be roped into being your assistant. From what I heard, I feel like Niccola and Andrea both spent most of their lives assisting *you*, looking for Methods for the reanimation. And I don't blame you or them. I expect they were adults with their own opinions, that made their own choices, but I just wanted to work unobserved by you." He must actually be taking this seriously to bring up his older siblings. They had been much older than Luca and had chosen to retire to have their own families and lives.

Luca held a hand down on the shoulder of the corpse which was still seizing, but continued like he did this every day. "Charlie actually said something when I was a kid. He said, 'Even though all the chimera were made by the same person and were iterations on a process, they weren't all the same and each had independent drives and interests. 'How' didn't determine 'what'.

"I took that to heart, and it led me to my own research. Well, that and the number of times you invited Emmanuelle Charpentier to dinner."

Elena responded, "Emanuelle is a brilliant woman. Why wouldn't we have dinner together?"

"Sure, but you two just seemed to talk about people you both knew. But I also remember you spending a fair bit of time in the kitchen trying to demonstrate you were able to cook, when you *never* cook. She and I spent a lot of time talking about CRISPR advances and applications."

Elena smiled like a cat in the cream. "Is that so? Emanuelle is a dear friend, and I'm glad you found her visits edifying."

Luca's brow furrowed, and Charlie imagined he must be putting the obvious clues together to realize that his mother had gotten him informal tutoring from a Nobel prize-winning scientist when he was a teenager and had stopped listening to his mother. Family fairy politics seemed to be taking the day.

Luca shook it off and said, "That aside, I've been collaborating with other scientists. Mostly other Quarterlings, but some out-of-House people too. And I think we're making progress on this. The chimera have been antsy for years to get out into the world physically instead of just participating in it virtually, and I told Charlie a while ago that they didn't need to live under the rectifiers to keep going. I know you noticed that their lifespan increased inside the enclaves, and that's a great reason to *keep* the enclaves active. But periodic recharges should work just fine and, not to compare you to a mouse, Charlie, but when the mice were socialized more they lived even longer."

Luca paused to let it sink in with his mother. The new chimera had stopped seizing, and Luca moved to hold their hand. Charlie had a dim first memory of someone holding his hand. He couldn't remember if it was Elena or Andrea. Real full consciousness took a few days, but the body liked to be comforted, even if the mind wasn't ready yet.

Charlie had planned to distract her with a few new details that seemed relevant now, so he took over and said, "I know you probably would have liked to know this sooner, but the chimera talk. It seems like those of us that were created with the same power source seem to have a more similar...I guess...'chimera experience'? The old lightning-born varieties just all seem to clique together, but we thought that was because they were generationally closer. Like from the same decades, same formative experiences.

"I didn't really remember how I was created, but I just naturally gravitated to some people and we didn't have much in common, even our ages, but I found out they were all hydroelectric chimera, so I did a little research. And since my donor's death was in the papers it seemed to line up with a trip you took."

Elena's eyes were tracking back and forth, and she said absently, "I remember, of course. Hoover Dam. It was a special project." She looked at him apologetically. "You know I waited on your mods until later, when I understood how to make the changes invisibly. Reanimating a recognizable musician, it was an opportunity to demonstrate the safety of the process." The corner of her mouth tugged down briefly. "I was hoping when House Shelley was finally in the public eye that you would be the spokesperson for the other chimera. I just thought nobody could look at you and want to start a mob. Well, maybe like a fan mob, but not a burn-you-to-death mob."

This wasn't news to Charlie. It had been mentioned to him that he, too, was evidence of Elena's weakness for a handsome face. Her plans and desires were always written large for anyone to see once they knew her. He wasn't really looking forward to the extra work, but he felt good about work done to help his fellow chimera.

Charlie said, "Then don't you think we should take House Shelley out into the world? You should probably use me while I'm still around. Chimeras may not age like normal people, but the fairy magic doesn't last forever."

Elena's eyes got glassy and started to leak tears at the corners. "It's not magic; it's science. I just don't understand the science yet. Are you feeling your time?" Some chimera just got tired and stopped. It wasn't involuntary exactly; they just wound down, like cell senescence or something. It was a thing you could feel coming on. Anyone who fought it off seemed to recover, but some chimera didn't fight it. Charlie could see a time when he'd like to be done, but not until he'd won a DAG award, at the least. And maybe not until Elena had her Method.

Charlie weighed his words. "I could use a change. I don't feel like I've been contributing to our House in any way I feel satisfied with. Feeling like eye-candy up on a shelf has worn thin."

"I don't have to go to the DAG awards. I can wait and give you as much time as possible before we're discovered. Everyone who left is trying to stay under the radar to make this as easy as possible. It could take years before any of them are caught. But House Shelley has changed and is going to change more. I've been following Luca's work, and it feels like an opportunity for growth.

"I feel like we've been in the shadows of the rectifiers for decades now, and it definitely hasn't been all bad. All the kids that came out of the rectifier animations are such smart cookies. They're bright and interested in the world, forward-minded. It's like those solar powered satellites sent the actual sunshine down for them and not just microwaves. But ultimately we're still in the shade. Literally, we live *in* the ground under a giant metal mesh. And I think we're all to the point where we could use a little sun." He looked over at Luca for help to push her over the finish line.

Luca let go of the hand in the tank and walked over to their cluster of chairs. Charlie stood and let Luca slide onto the stool next to his mother. Luca said, "Charlie is either exceptionally modest or unaware of his natural eloquence." Charlie turned away from such praise, even though it wasn't being said specifically *to* him, and as a natural extension of the movement he approached the gel tank.

He thought maybe it was *his* time to offer comfort, a hand to hold. He glanced quickly over at Elena and Luca, but neither of them were paying attention to him, and he could tell Luca had segued into a science run-down. So he slid his hand in the gel and felt a jolt. He continued anyway and grasped the new chimera's hand. The hand gripped his back though their eyes didn't open. He started to feel like he had while the switch was on and the rectifier electricity was overtaking the room. But he didn't mind, and he let the feeling evolve like a slow burn.

The chimera had been frugal with the details they let out to Elena. She always showed the signs of burning the candle at both ends, and he had watched her work herself to death once. Even though she came back and recovered her memories easily, it had been neither fun nor pretty to watch.

After that, there had been a conclave among all the different chimera enclaves, and they had all decided to limit the information flow so that Elena would work at a sustainable pace. Luca was so much like his mother. The chimera knew she felt she was the only one that could do the work and that obligated her to do as much work as super-humanly possible. Some chimera had even trained in science just to help her, but it still was too much for one person.

Charlie tuned back into the pitch Luca was making and heard Luca say, "… it's just the truth. Collaboration is the fastest way to advance towards a Method. I've been building a coalition of Quarterlings who are at loose ends, because their Houses have proven their main Method.

"They're all eager to work on fairy projects and use the skills they've developed to identify a Method. It's literally what most of them trained their whole lives to do, and now they're obsolete without a trick to work on.

"So I've been working with them, and it's been good. We've got next-level NDAs, because House Shelley isn't out; but we're making progress. I'd love to show you our data."

Charlie knew that was the best hook they were going to get, so he interjected with the real question. "Elena, our people have gone out into the world. Are we going to protect them?" She had turned to him and he could see the anxiety written large on her face.

He pushed her buttons intentionally before continuing, "Are we going to let them be rejected? You've been making the chimera resistant to the environments we're seeing from climate change. I know you want to be able to do it for living humans, too. To make sure people can live where their ancestors are from. Are you going to continue to do this on your own? There is more we could do with the resources to pursue parallel avenues. What are we going to do? House Shelley isn't a House without a Halfling, so we can't do it without you."

Elena gave him a resigned, sad look, "Are you sure you can't do it without me?" Charlie could tell that she had seen the shape of their revolt and was not unaware of the source of the pressure.

Luca responded, standing behind her and putting his hands on her shoulders. "We would never want to do it without you. No one could replace your expertise on this particular subject, and I've spent half my life not talking about my work with you. I'm ready to make family dinner interesting again. I know your lack of enthusiasm is due to sleep deprivation, not a lack of passion for doing the work."

Elena smiled fondly up at her son, "Look at you, all in charge. Give me twenty-four hours to sleep, and then I guess we get to have a press conference." Luca bolted from the room before she could change her mind, or maybe he was trying to make it back to his lab for his two-hour window.

Elena glared at Charlie and added, "You seemed to have things remarkably well planned. Did you have a plan for me joining your revolution?"

Charlie replied sincerely, "We *only* had a plan for you joining us. We know you. We've gone out into the world, but we need you to bring the world in."

Elena smiled; flattery worked better when it was true. She asked, "Do you have a date for the DAG awards?"

Charlie let out a choked laugh. The part of him that knew this was all going to end in tragedy finally relaxed, which was when he remembered that he should tell Elena about the interesting effect of being in the room with a new re-animation. But not until after the DAG awards. "It appears I do."

Athena Foster lives in the woods of Wisconsin rooting up faerie rings, writing speculative fiction, and performing bureaucromancy during the week. She studied creative writing at the Universities of Iowa and Wisconsin, and at last report is defending her 19th century farmhouse against a colonizing horde of pernicious woodchucks.

Raise Hell

Miranda Suri

*N**ico Slade: Present Day. Figueroa Street, Los Angeles. Summer.*
      There's an electric L.A. sunset smearing the sky like a toxic leak. I watch it through the double-tint of Aviators and smoked glass as my limo slides down the boulevard. On the corner, I spot the Four Horsemen smoking weed and drinking Jim Beam.

No one else can see them. Not yet.

I consider giving them a jaunty wave, for old times' sake, then think the better of it. I've learned the hard way that you don't play games with the Four Horsemen.

The car purrs around the corner, leaving them in the rearview. One more turn and we're there. The limo pulls to the curb and I stub out my Cuban in the ashtray.

Showtime.

Flanked by bodyguards, I exit the back to the eruption of flashbulbs. The paparazzi trailing the car are on me in seconds.

My hired muscle shove people back. A high-pitched whine, loud as a plane engine warming up, rises from the mob waiting outside the concert venue. They're all here for me, Nico Slade.

They're here for my voice. For the sound of jungle drums in the night. For fire, for ever-burning fire.

They're here to raise Hell on earth, but they don't know that. Not yet.

They don't know what they're listening to when I sing. They just know they can't stop.

The Horsemen have followed the limo.

They're across the street now, keeping tabs. The rider of the Pale Horse gives me a thumbs up. I turn away, remembering the last time I saw Death up here in the light.

Remembering when he came for me.

The pavement bakes in the late afternoon sun. Heat burns through the soles of my cowboy boots. It makes me think of home, of Hell and Texas--back when I wore a different body--and I smile.

I breathe deep. The crowd smells of the city. Of exhaust and urine. Of flop sweat, pot, and stale beer.

Then I stop. Under all that, I smell something else. Fresh earth. Graveyard earth.

The necromancer.

After her last attempt, in Cincinnati, when I'd sung her soul into submission and left her clutching her blade and her talismans and babbling this body's old name, well, I thought I'd seen the last of her then.

It chills me to think she's gotten this close without my noticing. She's a nobody, really, but she keeps coming, keeps playing my game, and I wonder if maybe I haven't been as clever as I thought. A shiver claws my spine, but I push my up sunglasses and pretend not to notice.

A lesson I learned in Hell: show madness or anger. Show cruelty or lust. But never, ever show fear.

The guards usher me past the crowd and the stage door shuts behind us with a bang. For an instant I'm in the dark.

I, Nico Slade, am in the dark.

And Nico Slade doesn't like being in the dark.

§

Two Years Earlier: East Texas

Garrett's fingers continued their downward trajectory after his final strum. The chord fell away, swallowed by the din in the bar.

No one seemed to notice. Some jackass had turned on the juke box halfway through the last set. Joan Jett had drowned out Garrett's ode to lost love and Def Leopard had blared over his gritty homage to Janis Joplin.

A crumpled beer can landed onstage, not far from the worn tips of his cowboy boots. His throat burned from growling into the mic. His T-shirt was sticky with sweat.

He was killing himself up here, and for what? He'd never get what he wanted like this.

Disgusted, he made his way offstage, trying not to dwell on all the years he'd slaved in dives like this one, hoping for a break.

Donnie McLaren waited in the dingy hallway, cigarette smoke clinging to him like mold on month-old bread.

"Garrett, my man. Killer set." Donnie's voice was oil and lies.

Garrett shrugged.

Donnie produced a fat wad of cash and peeled off four twenties. The bills were damp to the touch. Garrett stuffed them in his pocket as fast as he could, remembering how he'd gotten this gig in the first place, how Donnie's fingers had thumbed more than damp bills.

"Next weekend?" Garrett asked, trying not to sound desperate.

"Booked up next weekend." Donnie offered a sad shake of his head. "Weekend after too."

Garrett knew the brush-off. He scowled.

"You got the voice, my man. You do. But maybe work on some new material, yeah?" Donnie's eyes traveled Garrett with a lazy full-body caress. "Anytime you just wanna come hang out, though, that's cool."

"Yeah, man. Whatever." Garrett pushed past him, down the hall, boots squicking as they trod years of spilled booze and spit and Garrett knew all too well what else.

The night was hot, the kind of heat that never dissipates, that presses insistent against your skin, into your mouth, down your throat. Garrett crossed the lot, stepping over a pile of vomit cooling in the gravel, and yanked his truck door open.

Enough.

Enough of this bullshit.

It was time to go see Sharna.

§

Sharna turned her music up loud and took a long drag off her cigarette.

The bass line pounded into her. She lay on the sofa and imagined hands reaching from the speakers to pull her through to the other side.

It almost made her feel like she wasn't alone.

It was past three a.m. when headlights hit her driveway and glinted off the shingle posted on her door. She took a last pull from her cigarette. Reaching for the ashtray, she shoved aside a tangle of amulets and a dried-out stub of mandrake, then turned off the music.

The headlights went out and a car door slammed.

Sharna flicked the curtain aside and peered out. Though she hadn't seen it in a long time, she recognized the truck. Desire flared, followed by a slap of self-loathing.

Steeling herself to face him didn't make it any easier when she yanked the door open on Garrett Green.

Her beautiful loser.

At least, that's what her friends always called him.

A white v-neck tee clung to his chest, damp in the hot Texas night. Tattoos peaked from beneath the sleeves, climbing his biceps. She smelled smoke and cheap whiskey on his skin and wanted to lick it off.

"Sharna." His voice was low and musical, a beautiful voice. It should have made him famous, but it hadn't.

"What do you want?" She'd meant the words to come out hard rather than hopeful.

"I need your help."

Longing leapt in her chest with a desperation that made her sick. She schooled her features in disdain. "Solo career not workin' out? Well, too bad. My sticks aren't for sale anymore."

"I'm not looking for a drummer, Sharna. I'm looking for a necromancer. I want to raise a spirit."

"What? Why?"

He jerked his chin toward her shingle. "Says fifty bucks an hour, no questions asked."

She hesitated, knowing she'd probably regret this, but not wanting him to leave. "Fine. It also says fifty bucks upfront."

He pulled a handful of wadded bills from his jean's pocket and stuffed them in her hand. They were moist. Sharna shivered.

'Nothing to lose' was coming off Garrett in great, stinking waves.

"What gives? You in trouble?"

His eyes, usually so ready to make promises they couldn't keep, gave nothing away. His jaw clenched. His face closed down.

"You must be," she said, "if you're wanting to raise the dead after what happened last time."

He flinched, but said nothing.

She shrugged. "Alright, then. Where and when?"

"Matagorda Cemetery. Tomorrow night." He hesitated. "What time? Midnight?"

She nodded. It might be a cliché, but it really was the best time for raising spirits.

He stuffed his fists back in his pockets. "Midnight. Okay. See you then."

Sharna watched him go, thought about calling out, then thought the better of it. Garrett's lean body hunched as he walked to the pickup. She recognized the stance. She'd seen it when he'd told the band he was leaving the band and she'd seen it when he'd said he was leaving her.

Garrett Green had steeled himself for something and Sharna knew there'd be no talking him out of it.

She went inside and turned her music back on.

§

Garrett waited for Sharna outside the wrought-iron gate. The moon wasn't much more than a sliver. He wondered if that was good or bad for necromancy, then decided he wasn't sure he wanted to know.

The night smelled of dust and decay and his own cologne. He told himself he hadn't put it on for Sharna, but he'd been surprised when he'd seen her the night before. He'd forgotten her hard, waifish beauty, her dark-rimmed eyes and long waves of hair, the way she smelled of fresh earth.

Graveyard earth, he reminded himself. Death.

He heard the growl of her motorcycle coming down the lonely highway long before he saw her. She pulled up in front of the gate and flipped down the kickstand.

She wore cut-off jeans and a white tank top. No helmet.

"Hi," he said, which sounded lamer than he liked.

"You sure about this?" she asked.

"Are you?"

"I'm here, aren't I?"

He smiled, remembering another thing he'd forgotten. Sharna had always been willing to do anything for him.

She unslung her knapsack. "Clock starts now. Fifty bucks an hour."

Cicadas sang. It was a warm, dry night. A good night for beers by the river with a pretty girl. For a moment Garrett considered forgetting about spirits and just sweet-talking Sharna.

Then he thought about his career. About what he deserved. What he needed.

He pulled fifty bucks from his pocket and handed it to her.

"Okay," she said. "Let's go."

Garrett led her under the iron gate and into the graveyard, cowboy boots scuffing in the dust. Sharna followed, wending among the headstones.

He kept count of them in his head.

The grave was just where the internet had said it would be, thirteen rows back, fifth headstone from the end.

In life, Julia Raven been remarkable, a rocker destined for the Hall of Fame – or Hell. In death, all that paid homage to her was a generic marble stone with a few beer cans kicking around its base.

Julia Raven, the headstone read. Died age 21. R.I.P.

He wondered if she was resting in peace. She certainly hadn't in life.

Sharna stood beside him and stared at the headstone. "Garrett–" she began.

"I just want to talk to her."

She turned to him, dark eyes unreadable. "I don't understand. Why would you want to talk to the spirit of this crazy bitch?"

"She wasn't a bitch, and she wasn't crazy. Well, maybe a little, but in a genius kind of way. If she'd lived, she'd have been a rock legend."

Sharna pursed her lips, maybe remembering the one time their band had opened for Julia, maybe remembering the blood on the stage and Julia's insane, wild, beautiful laugh.

"Yeah, but she didn't live. She drove her band's bus off a cliff and killed them all."

"I'm sure she didn't mean it to go like that. It was a game. Just a game."

"Who plays games like that?" Sharna took a step back. "No. I don't like this. This isn't worth fifty bucks an hour."

Garrett closed his fingers around her arm, felt the warmth of her pulse beneath soft skin. "Wait. Come on, Sharna."

She froze under his touch. Deer in the headlights. Heartbeat fast. Garrett had forgotten this too. Forgotten his power over her. He swallowed and pulled her closer, close enough to see her lips tighten as she tried to make herself resist, close enough to see the gleam of amulets dangling against her cleavage.

"Please. I need this. I just want to talk to her."

"Why?"

"You know why. She had it, Sharna. Raw talent. Charisma." He leaned closer. "I've got the voice. Everyone says so. But I don't have that *thing*, that magical thing that makes you a star. Julia did."

Indecision wormed across her face. He trailed his fingers to her hip. "Please, baby. If I can just talk to her, learn her secrets…"

Sharna snorted. "What makes you think she'll tell you anything? Spirits don't care about the living, Garrett. You know that."

He shivered, remembering what had happened the last time Sharna had raised a spirit for him, the last time she'd tried to bring back the dead.

His mother. Her body stiff on the floor of their trailer. Her hands hard little claws around a bottle of Jack. Her eyes bulging from when she choked to death on her own sick.

"Please," he'd begged Sharna that night, like a fool. "Please bring her back. Just for a minute. I need to say goodbye."

She hadn't wanted to do it. She hadn't. But he'd convinced her in the end. After all, Sharna never could say no.

But his mother…

He closed his eyes. Her spirit had already been to Hell, and she hadn't wanted a tearful reunion. No. She'd possessed Sharna's body and tried to do things Garrett didn't want to remember.

He'd broken up with Sharna after that. That very night. Left her and left the band and never looked back.

Until now.

Sharna was watching him, and he knew she was remembering too, that in spite of everything she still loved him.

"It's not worth it," she said quietly. "You never get what you think you will from the dead."

He didn't meet her eyes. Couldn't. "That's my problem, not yours."

She frowned and he realized she really might change her mind. Really might not do this thing for him.

"Come on," he let a little desperation leak through. "Anything. I'll do anything. Maybe we could even get the band back together. We could get everything back, like it was before."

Lying, Garret found, got easier the more you did it.

"Please, baby. I need this."

Sharna closed her eyes. He had her.

"Okay," she whispered. "This once."

Yes.

"But we do it my way, by my rules. I call her and bind her. You stay outside the circle the entire time and you only get fifteen minutes, that's it."

Sharna moved as she spoke, unloading supplies, sprinkling some kind of powder around the grave, murmuring as she ran her fingers over her amulets.

Garrett nodded, not really listening. This was it. This was *it*.

He took a deep breath and thought about Julia Raven. The raw, snarling power of her performances had been a living thing. Every time she'd opened her mouth it had stripped something from his soul, left him desperate for more. He craved that, yearned to move people until they'd do anything, *anything*, to hear him sing again.

"Garrett, did you hear what I said?"

Sharna had a hand on one hip. Streaks of dust smudged the white of her tank top. She held a knife in her other hand. It was curved and serious-looking.

"What?"

"I'm about to call her. Are you ready?" She was all business now.

Garrett wet his lips. Was he ready? He nodded, suddenly unsure.

Sharna raised the knife to her arm. Garrett looked away. He heard a sharp intake of breath and knew her blood was dripping on the grave. First the offering. Then the summons.

Sharna sang the spirit forth.

Fear wormed through Garrett as if he were a rotten apple. Seeing Sharna work again was harder than he'd thought. And this, this moment when she sent her voice down to Hell, was another reason he'd left her.

Sharna's voice was pure. Like honey in the sunlight. And when she sang, you couldn't help but lean forward, draw closer, want more. Garrett hated her a little for that.

It wasn't fair. She didn't want to be a singer. Didn't want to do much other than play drums and raise the dead and love him.

If he'd had what she did, he wouldn't need to make a desperate bargain under a midnight sky with a long-gone spirit.

Breathe, he though. Focus. It's almost time.

Sharna's song twisted, the pitch rising, the melody doubling back on itself, splitting just as the earth at her feet split.

Julia Raven's spirit burst from the grave in a shower of earth and maggots and music. Her voice rang, the sound of a sunset on the last day at the end of the world, fire raining from the sky.

Garrett gaped at her. At the wild cloud of blonde hair surrounding her bruised face. At the pure, sick madness in her eyes as they fixed on him.

Her spectral hands were empty, but he remembered the bottle of Jim Beam she'd always had in concert, the slosh of amber liquid as she'd staggered across the stage. The smell of rage and sour stomach.

He stepped forward.

"Garrett," Sharna snapped. "Stay put."

He didn't, though. Couldn't. He crossed the circle, breaking Sharna's protective charms, ignoring her screams and the way her body slumped to the ground.

Julia's lips curved into a devil's smile.

He'd meant to bargain with her, to lay out an offer she couldn't help but find appealing. In exchange for her secrets, he'd unbind her spirit. He'd read a few books on necromancy at the library; he thought he knew how to do it.

He'd be a rock god and she'd be free. Win-win.

But as Julia Raven's spirit pinned him to the Texas dirt with nothing but her gaze, Garrett realized his plans didn't mean a damn thing.

§

Julia Raven stretched out one arm, then the other. Skin squeaked and protested. He was taller than she was, the boy whose body she'd claimed, and his muscles hung heavier off the bone than she was used to. Laughing, Julia puffed her chest out. It was flat and lean, and something stirred between her legs, hot and horny.

She was a man, a fucking *man*.

This body fit like new leather pants, stiff and stubborn in all the wrong places. But that would change. It would stretch and bend and break until its skin was a glove for hers.

The boy's soul nattered, though. It squirmed at the edge of Julia's consciousness, whining like a mosquito on a humid night.

She ignored it and looked down at the necromancer, nudging her unconscious body with a boot-clad toe.

The girl had called her up from Hell, up from a pool of fire, up from the molten daggers of the Devil's bed, up from the dark. And though Julia hadn't minded fucking the Devil one bit, she'd never liked being in the dark. This necromancer had freed her, at least, from that.

Julia had tasted the girl's blood offering and followed the echoes of her summoner's song from deep down below. She knew the necromancer loved the boy whose body she'd claimed. Loved him past reason. If she didn't kill her, the necromancer would come after her.

Julia mused on this.

The world had been a disappointment when she'd been alive, so craven and dull. She could change all that now, though. She could call up the damned with her song and give them bodies of their own.

This little necromancer would try and stop it. She would try and save the boy Julia had taken for a cheap costume, try to save him and this worthless world as well.

It would be a game, Julia decided. Yes, a game. A dance.

What fun they'd have!

Julia shivered with anticipation, wondering who would win. Would the necromancer send her back down into the dark or would she sing Hell up into the light?

As Julia smiled, she felt her strange new lips stretch and tear. Blood trickled at the corner of her mouth. Salty and real.

A man's lips. A musician's.

She'd need a new name. A rock star name.

Humming, Julia Raven stepped over the necromancer's body and walked into the Texas night.

§

Sharna: Present day. Figueroa Street, Los Angeles. Summer.

I clench my hand around the knife as I sniff out the trail Nico Slade left when he slithered through the crowd.

No, not Nico Slade. Julia Raven. Garrett Green.

I push forward with the surge of the crowd. They are eager to get inside. Hungry for the music.

I stop and lean against the rough concrete wall. My amulets are cold against my skin. I remember the last time they felt this way, when I lay naked on a sofa with Nico Slade in Cincinnati, thinking it was Garrett, believing I'd reclaimed his soul at last. Believing I'd won.

I want to cry, remembering how good that had felt, and how awful, after, when I realized I'd only lost again. Again and again.

I need the amulets to burn now, to burn me awake with their cold fire. But they've been inert for days, ever since I saw the Four Horsemen following me down Sunset.

I'd run from them and they'd laughed, not even bothering to give chase. They'd *laughed*.

I know what that means. I'm nothing, a bug. And Nico's winning. Always winning.

My palms are slick. The knife slips.

"Garrett Green," I whisper. To free Garrett. To save my beautiful loser. To save them all.

But deep down I know Garrett's gone and has been for a long time. Lost. I know they're all lost. Lost to the dark. They just don't know it yet.

I snarl as the person behind me shoves forward. But I'm not really angry. I understand. Even though I hate myself for it, I want inside too. I want to hear Nico Slade sing. I crave the sound of his voice. Garrett's voice, but more electrifying than Garrett ever was.

Garrett's voice with Julia's charisma is flame. It's the sound of the sunset on the last day at the end of the world, with fire raining from the sky.

And that's what Nico has brought, what I've brought. I opened Julia's grave and Hell spilled forth.

I have to find the strength to fix this, to stop her.

I drag a breath, first one, then another, and wonder how much longer I can hold on.

Tightening my grip on the knife, I allow the tide of bodies to carry me inside. The music shivers under my skin.

It's a Siren's song, and I follow.

Inside, the concert is getting underway. Nico's on the stage, tight white T-shirt plastered damp against Garrett's abs, lips nuzzling the mic, lights burning red on his tattooed skin.

I press forward and the crowd parts. Or maybe not. Maybe I imagine it. The room pulses to the beat of the drums. Jungle drums.

Nico Slade seduces us all. The eyes of the dammed peer from faces in the crowd and I sway. I sway with them.

A new song, and somehow I'm at the edge of the stage. How long have I stood here?

Nico smiles from above as if we're alone, the only two people in the universe. But there aren't just two of us. There are three: me and Garrett and Julia.

Or four: the Devil. Or five, six, seven, eight: the Four Horsemen. They ride across the stage, drunk and laughing.

Why can no one else see them? Or maybe they can.

The room blinks in and out with each heartbeat, each drum beat. Sweat runs down my back, between my breasts. My amulets are cold. The only cold thing left in the world.

The crowd pushes me up and I'm onstage. Nico pulls me close and the crowd wails and the drums, the drums, the drums.

The Four Horsemen dance. And fire. Ever-burning fire.

Nico tries to kiss me. Does he kiss me? Do I kiss him back?

I'm crying, and finally my amulets burn.

I raise my knife. I raise my voice and sing.

I sing for my life. For Garrett's. For the world.

I sing.

Miranda lives in Seattle, Washington, where she writes speculative fiction, raises her young son, and gardens. Her writing has appeared in publications such as Psuedopod, Flash Fiction Online, Penumbra, Every Day Fiction, and Electric Spec, among others. Her short stories *The Firefly Girl* and *What We Found* were included in Tangent Online's recommended reading list and The Best of Abyss and Apex, respectively. You can learn more about Miranda at www.mirandasuri.com

HOUSE OF THE GREMLIN

Shannon Ryan

I woke up to a city worker poking me with a broom handle. I suppose this was only fair as he was driving a street sweeper, and I had slept in his street. I wondered how I had ended up in the predicament, though not for too long as the workman was still poking me.

I remembered a video call from Aunt Violet and flying in on the evening sub-orbital shuttle. My family somehow failed to take the hint that I lived on the other side of the planet in order to minimize fraternization. At the spaceport, I'd run into my old school chum, Cosgrove Pitt-Jones. Old PJ had invited me to the bar for a few drinks. Things got a little foggy after that, but I do remember stealing a bicycle at some point.

"Oi, you there! Get up and move along." The man prodded me again with his broom.

I groaned and tried to sit up, but the world spun around me. "Where am I?"

"You're in the gutter, mate. Now get up before I call the constable."

I stumbled to my feet and looked around. By the general appearance of things and the workman's accent, I guessed I was still in London. "What time is it?" I asked.

"It's nearly noon. Now get moving before I alert the authorities," the man repeated, clearly losing patience.

I stumbled away, still trying to piece together why my head felt like it was about to explode. The term "noon" wafted around the old bean, and it struck me like a ton of bricks that I was about to miss the appointed time for Aunt Violet's Sunday dinner, a treasonous offense. I looked around for a robotaxi but found none. If I arrived late to her townhouse, there would be hell to pay.

I spotted a bicycle parked nearby, possibly the one I'd stolen the previous night, and rushed to it. I hopped on and looked for the starter. Unfortunately, I had stolen a leisure model, with no self-drive capacity for rapid commuting, probably why it had been so easy to steal. Undeterred, I put my Oxfords to the pedals and propelled the two-wheeler ahead using just the power of my feet.

I was quite winded by the time I piloted the cycle onto Aunt Violet's lawn. Still, I stopped to put down the kick stand--I could see her peering out from behind the curtains, a scowl on her face. I rushed inside, knowing I had cut the minutes quite short despite my efforts. "My dear Aunt Violet," I said, trying to catch my breath.

Aunt Violet wore a dark blue dress with red accents and gold buttons. With her matching hat and disapproving look, she was a dead ringer for Napoleon about to give the troops a good dressing down. "You're red in the face, and you look like you've been in a brawl," she said scrutinizing my appearance. "I hope you have a good excuse, Victor Barclay Beckham." She only used my full name when she was annoyed. She usually called me Vicky like most of my friends.

I thought quickly, trying to come up with something to appease her, and as I often did, I lied. "I was on a secret mission for the government, and I can't tell you anything about it."

There was a quite funny story about that. A few years ago, at one of her dinners, she announced that I needed to get a job. Typically, when Aunt Violet makes a proclamation, I try to play along, as she controls one-third of my trust fund, along with her sisters. Of course, a job seemed too far beyond the thingy. In my panic, I told her the first thing that popped into my head--I had a very important government job, but I couldn't tell her anything about it. Of course, for my cover, it was important to maintain my lavish and carefree way of life. Over the years, details had been added, leaving me in an ever-contracting web.

Aunt Violet looked me up and down. "Well, that explains the condition of your clothing. Why don't you go freshen up a bit?

Colonel Clarke is running late, so you have a little time."

It seemed to me that if Clarke was running late, she hadn't really been justified in reading me the riot act, but as the bard said, *The better part of valor is* whatever, so I held my tongue. Apparently very close friends were given more latitude than nephews. I had long suspected Clarke of being my aunt's secret paramour. Despite their close association, however, they had always maintained the utmost decorum.

Reggie, Aunt Violet's person assistant, appeared by my elbow as if by magic and guided me into a guest room. I'd always liked Reggie, he had quite the head on his shoulders as well as the proper deferential loyalty you so rarely see in servants these days. "If you leave your clothes, sir, I will do my best to repair them. You may wish to avail yourself of the en-suite shower. I find nothing beats the refreshing sensation of a good scrub, sir."

"Do you think I really need one, Reggie?"

As he carefully folded my discarded vestments, he said, "Pardon me for being forward, sir. I couldn't help but notice that your olfactory essence seems to be somewhat...pungent."

Sometimes I find Reggie's word choices a bit odd, but I did perceive the aroma of his nub. "I suppose splashing around never hurt anyone."

"As you say, sir."

A short time later, I emerged from the shower, feeling quite refreshed. Atop the bed lay my attire, not precisely in mint condition, but more spruced up than when it had left my possession. On a small silver tray sat a glass of water and a couple of Recover hangover tablets.

As I returned to the drawing room, I heard Aunt Violet say, "Colonel, please, do come in. You'll have to excuse the disheveled state of my nephew. He's just returned from a very serious secret mission."

Clarke's eyes lit up. "Victor, my boy. I hadn't realized you'd entered government service. It's always good to meet a fellow agent in the espionage game." He tapped the side of his nose.

I froze for a moment, unsure of how to respond, snared in my fabrications. As I mentioned earlier, I certainly wasn't in the espionage game. I finally decided on, "Aunt Violet, you know I can't speak of those things."

Before I could say anything more, Aunt Violet cut in. "Yes, yes, Colonel. Vicky is one of the best in the business. I'm sure he'll have some fascinating stories to tell over dinner."

I decided I should have a nice stiff drink or two before dinner.

As we sat down to eat, Clarke questioned me about my supposed missions and adventures. The pre-dinner libations mingled with the strong wines, both table and dessert, generously provided by Aunt Violet. By the end of dinner I was telling wild stories about protecting the realm from the King's enemies both home and abroad.

After dinner, Clarke and I sipped cognac in the library. I was falling into a warm Sunday afternoon drowsiness, when Clarke said, "Victor, my boy, I don't know if you've heard about this nasty business with the lunar colonies."

"Well, I—" Weren't there terrorists, or separatists, or separatist terrorists up there? I always found it a good policy to steer well clear of those who would kill for their principles.

"Of course you have. Anyway, I've been looking for a man with just your skill set to do some information gathering for me."

My previously relaxed demeanor disappeared instantly. I had never been to the lunar colonies, and I knew nothing about the "nasty business" he was talking about. I tried to think of a way out, but before I could say anything, Aunt Violet walked in.

"Colonel, I hope you're not trying to steal my nephew away from me." She sounded both a bit amused and a bit miffed.

Clarke chuckled. "Not at all, my dear. I was just discussing a potential opportunity for Victor."

Aunt Violet's eyes narrowed. "I see. Well, I'm afraid Vicky is not available for any missions at the moment. I need him for a little project of mine."

Clarke looked disappointed, but he quickly recovered. "Of course, of course. I understand. I'll have to find someone else for the job."

I breathed a sigh of relief. I didn't want to go all the way to the moon. In the future, I had to be more careful about what I said. I couldn't keep making up stories. Still, everything had worked out for the best, safe and sound in Aunt Violet's library, sipping cognac and pretending to be a spy.

Clarke held my aunt's hands. "My dear lady, I'm afraid I must take my leave."

On his way to the door, the old man walked by and squeezed my elbow. He whispered. "Victor, we'll continue this conversation later. We need to get you to the moon." Even more softly, he said, "Elephants play chess, but squirrels play poker." Before I'd finished parsing that baffling sentence, he was gone.

When I heard the front door close, I turned to Aunt Violet. "Now, my wonderful Aunt Violet, you said you needed my help with something?" I expected she needed me to assist Reggie in shifting a table or some similar, manly endeavor.

"Did I tell you that your Uncle Rupert has been spending a lot of time at the country estate?"

"I wasn't aware as such." Never polite to mention that it was common knowledge a couple had not slept together in the marital bed for years.

"Well, your uncle has taken to collecting antique automobiles. In fact, he has joined the American Motor Company Collecting Club of Buckinghamshire and Bedfordshire."

I frowned. Uncle Rupert's latest hobby didn't sound like it was going to end well. He had a tendency to get carried away with his passions. I could already see a fleet of rusting, ancient wrecks haunting the grounds of his stately home. "I see," I said, trying to hide my concern. "And what do you need my help with?"

"I'm sure you know that your uncle and I don't always see eye-to-eye, and well, your uncle is thinking about selling this townhouse." There came the nub of her gist. She quite adored this particular townhouse as well as her neighbors, one of which was Colonel Clarke.

I pshawed. "I had no idea. I thought you lived in utter marital bliss."

She gave me a withering look. "Be serious, Vicky. I've decided to give him a special gift, the rarest collectible AMC vehicle, a little thing called a 'Gremlin.' Now, I've gotten you tickets on the next available transport, but you'll have to make plans to ship it when you arrange a deal."

"Arrange a deal? Tickets?" I sputtered. "Where exactly am I going?"

"There is a collector who just happens to have a mint condition Gremlin on the moon."

I groaned and leaned back in my chair. "The moon? Aunt Violet, I just got back from a secret mission, and now you want me to go to the moon? I hear the weather is horrible there this time of year." Again, I really had to stop lying about being an agent.

"Oh Vicky, stop being silly. You know the moon doesn't have an atmosphere."

Actually I hadn't, but I waited for her to continue.

"Now, I am counting on this gift. I need to show your uncle that I can at least make an effort at reconciliation."

I sighed. There was no getting out of it. "Very well, Aunt Violet. I'll leave tomorrow for the moon."

"Good boy, Vicky. I knew I could count on you."

I took another sip of my cognac, already regretting my promise. The moon. It was going to be a long trip.

"Now, I want you to be very firm with this collector, Jasper White. Don't go a penny over a half million. And I want you to take

Reginald with you."

I nearly spit out my cognac. "What?"

"Reginald," Aunt Violet repeated. "He's been feeling a bit cooped up lately, and I think the change of scenery will do him good. Besides, he'll be your personal assistant on this mission, and he's got a knack for these types of things. He's quite clever you know."

I sighed, knowing there was no arguing with Aunt Violet. "Fine, Reggie can come along."

Reggie, who had been hovering in the background, stepped forward. "Thank you, madam, sir. I shall prepare the necessary arrangements."

"Excellent," Aunt Violet said. "And Vicky, do try to stay out of trouble this time."

I scoffed. "Me? Get into trouble? Never."

§

The next morning, the Sun had got its hat on, and it seemed a shame to leave the planet on a day when God had blessed the green and pleasant land with a rare perfect day. However, time and tide and so on. I had an aunt to appease.

I'd come to London with only a few items of clothing, thinking I'd be back in the floating city of New Chicago by the evening. This necessitated the acquisition of some new attire and the luggage to stow it in. As I arrived at the spaceport, I was wearing a new, bright blue, shiny suit, an outfit the haberdasher had told me was all the rage in lunar circles. It made a slight crinkly sound when I moved, which was apparently part of the fashion. I had also purchased a pair of moon boots. They apparently did some complicated technical thingy so you could walk around on the moon without having to hop about like a kangaroo.

When I strolled into the station, a stiff, military-looking chappy immediately walked up to me. Despite his civilian dress, the bloke couldn't have looked more the part of a Royal Marine if he'd been wearing the uniform and standing by a recruiting poster. He pushed an envelope into my hand. "Elephants play chess, but squirrels play poker." Then the fellow bestowed upon me a conspiratorial wink. Before I could inform him where he might deposit his letter, he pivoted and strode away at a brisk pace. Nonplussed, I shrugged and tucked the missive into my pocket.

I spotted Reggie standing guard over my luggage. "Good morning, Reggie. I hope the day finds you well."

Reggie eyed my suit carefully, as if it might blind him if he stared too long. "Good morning, sir. I trust you slept well."

"I did, thank you. Have you seen our tickets?"

"Yes, sir. Unfortunately, there seems to have been an oversight. Your aunt booked us in third class seats."

Personally, I had no doubt the old bird did it on purpose to save herself a bit of coin. It was amazing how tight the dynastic wealthy could be sometimes. "And I supposed it's too late for an upgrade?" I looked at him hopefully, but Reggie responded with a sympathetic look. "Well, I suppose we must make do."

I sighed, resigned to the fact that I was going to be spending a long, uncomfortable journey to the moon in third class. "Let's get on board, Reggie. The sooner we get to the moon, the sooner we can get back."

We made our way to the shuttle, dodging porters and other travelers as we went. When we finally found our seats, I was disheartened to observe they were as cramped and uncomfortable as one might expect from third class. I settled in, trying to find a comfortable position, but it was no use. At least there was an empty seat in our row, and I was able to spread out a bit.

Unfazed by the cramped quarters, Reggie pulled out a tablet and started typing, completely ignoring the chaos around us.

With a "bing-bong" chime, the screens on the seat backs lit up, warning us to take our seats. I closed my eyes and tried to relax. I was in for a long journey.

"Excuse me," someone said.

I opened my eyes to see a rather curvaceous, middle-aged woman leaning down to me, putting me at eye level to her immense cleavage.

She held out her hand for me to shake. "Maggie Campbell," she announced.

I took her hand, slightly flustered by her close proximity. "Pleased to meet you, good lady. I am Victor, and this is my assistant Reggie."

Maggie beamed at us. "It's such a pleasure to meet you both." She nodded to the empty seat between us. "So, do you mind if I take my seat?"

I was momentarily ruffled both that I had missed her social cues and that we were about to lose our little bit of privacy—I had assumed having the first and third seat in the row meant the middle one would be empty. "Of, course, my good lady. I apologize." I stood and helped her into her seat.

"You are a toff one, aren't ya, 'my good lady.' Don't worry your little head, handsome. No offense taken." Maggie and I squashed ourselves into the limited space. My suit made many crinkly noises, and I became acquainted more closely with Maggie's contours. I tend to run slim, as do most of the Beckhams, but Maggie's physique made one want to bandy about terms like robust and ample.

Once we were well in the air and headed away from the planet, I saw the bar cart coming down the aisle and decided that even if I couldn't update my seat, there was no reason to travel without a little liquid comfort. Not wanting to be rude, I turned towards Maggie, as much as possible within our constraining situation. "Could I offer you a glass of champagne?"

"Where do you think you are, luv? They don't even sell champagne to the likes of us. If you are lucky, they might have some swish." Swish was a beverage well loved by the lower classes, made from watered down fruit juices and pure grain alcohol. Maggie pulled a sizable flask from her ample bosom. "Here, have a nip of this."

Not wanting to show the woman disrespect, I took a swig from the proffered vessel and realized a taste not unlike an industrial cleaning solution. I swallowed hard and waited for the burn to subside. "Thank you, dear lady. A quite unique beverage."

Reggie, who had been observing the exchange with interest, spoke up. "Madam, may I inquire what is in that flask?"

Maggie beamed at Reggie. "It's my special recipe, a blend of the finest spirits and a secret ingredient. It's sure to keep you warm on this chilly journey to the moon.

As I was thinking that no trip to the moon could be chilly pressed so firmly against Maggie's ample form, she thrust the flask in front of Reggie. "Would you like a snort, Reggie?"

Reggie held up his hand to wave away the extended spirit. "I'm afraid, madam, that I am unable to partake at this time. I am here in a professional capacity, and I abstain from hard beverages while working."

Being refused by Reggie, the flask was passed back to me. I took another sip, trying to hide my grimace. However, I found to my amazement, that with re-sampling, the strange elixir was developing a certain charm.

As we chatted with Maggie, I started to relax and forget about my discomfort. She was a lively and entertaining companion, regaling us with stories of her travels and adventures, as well as those of her many sons, who were by all accounts as robust and adventurous as their mother. Before I knew it, we were laughing and having a grand time.

By the time we stopped at Lagrange One to let people off at Midpoint Station, I was feeling quite a bit tipsy. Maggie, on the other hand, seemed completely unaffected. She was still chatting away, her laughter ringing through the cabin.

§

We arrived at Armstrong City Spaceport without further incident. As we exited the shuttle, my suit making crinkling noises, I said to Maggie, "Dear lady, thank you for sharing your wonderful elixir. If you ever visit New Chicago, please call on me." For some reason, I was none too steady on my feet--probably the low gravity--so Reggie hired a couple porters to transport myself and our luggage to the Armstrong Hilton.

The next morning, I woke to a splitting headache. At least this time, I was in a five-star hotel, and not the gutter. I sat up in bed in time to find Reggie bringing in a tray with tea, toast, and a tablet showing the Armstrong City Times. He'd also been kind enough to include a couple of Recover tablets.

"I've laid out clothes for you," Reggie said, proving himself to be a provider of not only sustenance but couture.

I looked at the foot of the bed, where Reggie had laid out a very dark, conservative suit that I'd only packed in case of a funeral or state dinner. "I'm not sure about that choice. Rather drab isn't it? What about the red crinkly one?"

"I thought more conservative attire might prove to the collector, Mr. Jaspar White, that you are a serious buyer and not some kind of circus performer."

I opened my mouth to protest, but I stopped. Reggie had been awfully good bringing those Recover tablets. Perhaps I should allow him this indulgence. "Okay, Reggie. I shall trust your judgment."

"Very good, sir. I would advise you rise before luncheon. I've arranged a meeting. Mr. White has agreed to meet with us in the early afternoon."

I groaned and rubbed my temples. "Isn't it a little early to discuss business?"

"I apologize for the discomfort, but Lady Violet is counting on us to procure that automobile for your uncle."

I sighed, knowing he was right. "Very well, Reggie."

"I procured a lunar conveyance, so we can leave at your convenience."

I dismissed him with a commanding wave of a toast point. "Fine then. I'll be ready."

"Very good, sir. If I may be permitted to mention one further matter. While putting away your garments from yesterday, I discovered a small envelope in one of the pockets. I have taken the liberty of placing it beneath your newspaper, sir."

Reggie left the room, and I lay back in bed, trying to shake off the last vestiges of my hangover. I was on a mission to the moon, and I couldn't afford to let anything get in my way. But first, I needed another cup of tea.

I was well into my second cup of tea before I started to feel myself. I opened the envelope and read the note.

Vicky-

So glad to see you made it to the moon. Your targets are a group of separatists called the Emerald Enforcers. More information to follow.

-CC

P.S. Eat this note when you're done.

I imagined CC was short for Colonel Clarke. As far as I knew his given name was Matthew. I sighed and walked over to the toilet, where I flushed the note. The colonel might go in for such things, but I'd rather risk stopping up a toilet than being stopped up myself.

A few hours later, I was dressed and driving across the lunar surface in a moon buggy, quite similar to a luxury hovercar but outfitted with its own pressurized atmosphere and everything you needed to survive on the lunar surface until help could arrive. I gazed though the viewscreen, steering around the larger boulders, whilst marveling at the craters and mountains. "Tell me about this collector," I said to Reggie.

"Jasper White is a self-made businessman, famously as stubborn as he is protective of his collection."

"So he's going to be a tough nut to crack," I surmised.

"Indubitably, sir."

We pulled up to a large, domed mansion and docked at their airlock. I straightened my suit and tie and took a deep breath. It was time to put my negotiating skills to the test. As we entered the building, we were greeted by an attractive young woman. "Good afternoon, gentlemen. Uncle Jasper is waiting for you in the main showroom."

She led us down a long corridor and into a large, open area under the dome. Cars of all shapes and sizes were displayed in the courtyard, not my sort of thing, but I wasn't about to disparage a man's collection.

Jasper White was a rotund man with a thick, white mustache and a twinkle in his eye. He wore a white suit that was very shiny and extremely crinkly. He welcomed us with a firm handshake. "Gentlemen, it's a pleasure to meet you. I'm Jasper White."

"Delighted to make your acquaintance, old chap! My given name is Victor Barclay Beckham, but my friends call me Vicky." I said in my friendliest of tones.

White was right down to business. "Enough pleasantries, I understand you're here to discuss the acquisition of my Gremlin?"

I smiled, trying to put the man at ease. "Indeed, Mr. White. My uncle is a collector and he's quite taken with the idea of adding a Gremlin to his collection. My aunt wants to make it a gift."

"Well, I have one in mint condition, perhaps the highest quality specimen still available," Jasper said, leading us over to a small, green car. "However, it's a rare item, and I'm not sure I'm ready to part with it."

I took a deep breath and steeled myself for the negotiation. "Let me be perfectly frank with you, Mr. White." I beamed him my most charming grin. "What must I do to gain your favor?"

White thought about it for a moment and then he asked, "How old do you think I am?"

I feared this was a trick question, but I couldn't think of a better way to answer than with the truth. "Forty-five, maybe a tich older?"

"Sixty-seven." He grinned in delight at my answer. "That's the thing about living on the moon. Less gravity to pull at the wrinkles." He eyed me carefully. "And I assume you're about half my age?"

I nodded. I was actually a bit younger than that. "Give or take."

"Tell you what. I'm challenging you to a foot race, one lap around the inside of my dome. If you can beat me, you can have the Gremlin. If you can't, you can pound sand."

I pondered my choices. I couldn't help but think the man must have some secret advantage, but I was unable to determine what it could possibly be. In addition to being much older than me, he lacked a runner's physique. "All right, you're on."

From behind me, Reggie cleared his throat.

I held up a finger, "One momento, Mr. White." I turned to Reggie. "What is it?"

"I would advise against this wager, you see—"

"Oh, pish." I turned back to White. "All right, let's get started."

We shook hands on it and walked to the outside edge of the dome. I was feeling pretty confident until White had his niece bring him a pair of high-tech lunar racing shoes. I looked down at my formal moon boots feeling a bit disadvantaged.

Reggie dropped his handkerchief to start the race.

I jumped into action—quite literally. Forgetting to account for the gravity, I shot almost straight up and cracked my noggin against the dome, which was much closer to the ground out by the edge. I got up and tried again, but I was badly lagging behind. I tried to shuffle along in a quick walk, but White crossed the finish line long before I did.

I was sweating and panting by the time I made it to the finish line. White came over to me, a smug grin on his face. "Sorry, Vicky. Better luck next time."

I had to admit, I was disappointed. But I wasn't one to give up that easily. "Wait a minute. I have an idea." I called to White. "What if I beat you in a game of Lunar Poker?"

White shook his head. "Sorry, boy. What about 'pound sand' didn't you understand? You see, I didn't want to sell to you anyway. I looked up your uncle through my contacts. He's only been in the AMC collector's club for two years. Just another rich snob trying to buy his way in. I bought my first Pacer when I was only fifteen and refurbished it with my own two hands. You see, I'm a self-made man Mr. Beckham, and I'm a moon man. I have no time for a soft, privileged boy from Earth, who has the nerve to visit me wearing a non-reflective suit which doesn't even make noise."

My mouth must have gaped open for several seconds at the veracity of the man's rant. I thought the foot race a quirky diversion. I didn't realize White had done it to put me in my place and disparage my relatives. I was just about to give him a piece of my mind when Reggie took hold of my arm.

"Perhaps, sir, it's time to leave."

As he pulled me away, I turned and said, "Thank you for your time, White. I can't say it's been a pleasure." With that biting insult, I turned my back and walked to the main airlock.

As I drove back to the Armstrong Hilton, I quite magnanimously kept mum about Reggie's error in picking out my attire. Regarding the actual interaction with White, I felt my anger dissipate into frustration. I had been one footrace from acquiring the rare Gremlin for my aunt. And now, I would have to find another way to secure it.

"Blast it, Reggie. I really thought I could beat the old man in that foot race. I would have had him too, if he hadn't resorted to trickery."

"Indeed sir, a most ingenious stratagem, knowing the effects of lunar gravity. I did try to warn that while the engineering of lunar footwear has come a long way, your boots are made for walking, and that's just what they'll do."

"Oh well. I might as well tell Aunt Violet the bad news." I opened up a video screen and called Aunt Violet.

She answered voice only and said, "What do you want Vicky?

You know it's four in the morning in London?"

"Oh, so sorry. I just wanted to give you an update on the mission, *id est*, the procurement of the Gremlin. Unfortunately, things didn't go so well with Mr. White."

She was silent, and I thought she might be too mad to talk. I was working myself up to apologize profusely when she started to speak. "That's not acceptable, Vicky. Get that Gremlin. Steal it if you have to. I've already told your uncle I have a special surprise for him. I must have that automobile."

"Steal it?" I was aghast. "Aunt Violet, I can't do that. It's unethical."

Again, she paused. "Unethical? That's rich coming from you, Vicky. You're a spy. And now you're going to stand on principle? Get that Gremlin, Victor Barclay Beckham, or don't bother coming back to Earth." The video call ended, and I was left staring at the blank screen.

I glanced at Reggie for reaction and found nothing but the slight hint of an upturned eyebrow. "Well, Reggie, it looks like we're going to have to come up with a new plan."

Reggie nodded. "Indeed, sir. Perhaps we could try a different approach with Mr. White. A more... diplomatic tone."

I nodded, relieved that Reggie was on board. "Yes, that's exactly what we'll do. We'll show Mr. White that we're not like those other collectors. We'll earn his trust and show him that we're true enthusiasts."

Reggie nodded again. "Very good, sir. I'll start making arrangements for our next meeting with Mr. White."

"And what was that with Aunt Violet pausing for so long before speaking?"

"I think you'll find, sir, that we are over one light second from earth, when taking into account satellite routing, that means a three second round trip time for signals. From her perspective, she was the one waiting for you to speak."

I wasn't exactly sure what he'd just said, but it sounded damn technical, so I assumed it was correct. "Well, I think they should work on fixing that."

"I have no doubt someone is working on bypassing the light speed limitations, sir."

Just then, another video call came through, from Jaspar White of all people. Reggie put him up on the screen. Despite it being less than an hour since our negotiation, the man appeared thoroughly disheveled and visibly shaken, as if he had just gone through a tumultuous ordeal. Something behind him seemed to be on fire.

"Damn you, Beckham. If I find out you had anything to do with this desecration of my sacred refuge, this vicious attack on my treasured possessions, I will prosecute you to the fullest extent of the law. I am not without connections, you know."

I was taken aback by the man's sudden change of tone. "What are you talking about, White? What attack?"

"Mere moments after you left empty-handed, the so-called Emerald Enforcers broke through my dome, and took several valuable pieces from my collection." He was practically shaking with rage. "I don't consider it a coincidence that their arrival aligned so closely with your departure."

I was stunned. "Mr. White, I swear I had nothing to do with this. We just left your dome. This is the first I'm hearing about this attack."

"Then how do you explain the timing of these events?"

Reggie cleared his throat and leaned into the video window. "Mr. White, I hope you don't mind if I interject, but did the thieves take any interest in your Gremlin?"

That turned down his bluster a notch. "Well, no. It's a bit big to carry out…"

"In that case it behooves me to point out that the automobile in question was the only part of your collection that my employer cared about. This makes him a less than likely suspect."

White's eyes narrowed. "Sure, that's your take on it. I'll be keeping an eye on you, Beckham. I'm still not convinced of your innocence, and I'm all the more relieved I didn't let you get your grubby little hands on my Gremlin." And with that, he cut the transmission.

I looked at Reggie. "What do you make of all this?"

"The Emerald Enforcers have been known to target collectors like Mr. White. This seems to be an unfortunate concatenation of circumstance."

"And it seems like we're right in the middle of that concata…whats-it. You know, Reggie, there used to be an old saying, 'Mother said there'd be days like this.'"

"She did, sir? I did have the pleasure of knowing your mother."

"No, Reggie, that's the saying."

Reggie nodded. "Indeed, sir. It appears that the fates have not been kind to us on this occasion."

That evening, I sat in the parlor of my hotel suite, going through my correspondence. I'd made a few video calls, but with the light-speed whats-it to Earth, I'd opted for written replies to all but the most urgent communiques. Even as I was going through the flattered-by-your-kind-words and a-delight-to-hear-froms, something was nagging at the back of the old noggin.

"Say, Reggie. These Emerald Enforcers chaps who robbed White, weren't they the same fellows the colonel was prattling on about?"

"I could not say, sir. As I would never look through your private correspondence without your prompting. I do believe the note I found earlier in your ridiculous blue suit may have contained some information."

"Very little information. And leave my suit out of this." Having allowed Reggie the opportunity to feel ashamed for his slight against my attire, I resumed. "Half the note was an instruction to eat it. After a cursory examination, I consigned it to the depths of the WC."

"I don't suppose Colonel Clarke left you information on how to contact him or anyone else in the intelligence services."

I shrugged. "No, I suppose the old boy assumed I had my own such people since Aunt Violet told him I was such a great spy. I don't suppose I could just call him, could I?"

"I doubt it would be that easy, sir. Colonel Clarke has no doubt been using secretive and unconventional methods to contact you for a reason."

Just then, the doorbell rang. Reggie went to answer it and returned with a small, spindly robot. It was carrying a package wrapped in brown paper. "Delivery for Mr. Beckham," the robot said in a monotone voice.

I opened the package to find a tablet computer and a note.

The note read, "Use this device to contact me. Destroy after use." It was signed, "CC." Well, at least he hadn't wanted me to eat it.

I looked at Reggie. "I think we might have a lead." I activated the tablet and an image of Clarke appeared. "Good to see you made it to the moon, Beckham," Clarke said. "I have information on the Emerald Enforcers. They are a dangerous group and should not be taken lightly."

"I had managed to figure that much out on my own," I replied to the recording.

"According to our sources, the gang hangs out in a place called the Crater Cafe. I want you to go there, have lunch, be leisurely, take your tablet and do some reading. Just keep your ears open and see if you can find something out."

"Understood, Clarke," I said to the recording, before turning to Reggie. "Well, Reggie, it looks like we're off to the Crater Cafe." I looked up to see Reggie contemplating something. "Reggie, is there anything on your mind?"

"Yes, sir. It occurs to me that if you could negotiate a truce with the Emerald Enforcers, you could perhaps buy back the items from Mr. White's collection, ingratiating him to you and possibly reopening negotiations for the Gremlin."

I nodded enthusiastically, but I saw one issue with his plan. "But, Reggie, won't negotiating with such a notorious gang put us in peril?"

After considering for nary a moment, Reggie replied. "In that case, sir. I believe you should go on your own."

§

Around noon the next day, we made our way to the Crater Cafe, a dingy place located in the older, underground part of the city. After the debacle with White, I'd insisted that Reggie dress me in the shiniest and noisiest of my new suits.

As I strode into the cafe, I noticed a group of shady-looking characters huddled in the corner. The theme of the place seemed to be twentieth century Americana, so I ordered an iced tea and a hamburger. I took a seat at the lunch counter, and while I was waiting for my meal, took out a tablet and started to read the local newspaper.

Through the corner of my eye, I tried to watch the comings and goings of those around me, especially the corner booth with the rough characters.

"Vicky!" I heard someone yell. I turned to see Maggie from my shuttle ride. "Fancy meeting a toff like you in a place like this."

I nodded and said, "Well met. I was passing by this eatery, and I had a craving for an American-style hamburger. What brings you here, good lady?"

"I happen to own this establishment." She waved to the big, nasty customers taking up the corner booth. "Boys, come over here and meet Mr. Beckham."

As Maggie's boys approached, I felt a sudden pang of unease. They were large men, with cold eyes and unshaven faces. One of them even had an eye patch.

I tried to keep my cool and put on a friendly smile. "Pleased to meet you, gentlemen."

Maggie gave me a warm smile. "Mr. Beckham, these are my sons, Seth, Rueben, Adam, and Amos." Adam was the one with the eye patch. "Now, let me give you a tour of my little restaurant. Have you ever been inside a walk-in freezer before?"

"Funny of you to ask that, really. A few years ago, Head First Peterson and I--"

I never got to finish my story, as just then, Rueben and Adam grabbed me by my shoulders. My suit made a surprised noise. They slid me off my stool and marched me through the kitchen, past a cook standing at a stove which seemed to produce nothing but smoke and grease.

When we arrived at the aforementioned freezer, they thrust me inside, seated me on a chair, and trussed me up like a chicken. My tethering allowed me just enough slack to look around, more's the pity.

The walk-in freezer was the proverbial "nothing to write home about," unless of course, you were a food inspector. Grimy icicles hung from the ceiling, suspicious looking stains painted the walls, and wilted and rotting produce lounged around in heaps. I found myself positively taken aback by the state of the produce, given the rather exorbitant price of foodstuff on the moon. The only visual reprieve was the floor, which was obscured by a fine mist.

With Maggie and her sons watching me, I felt I should say something. "I'm not sure if I am a fan of lunar hospitality."

"Ask him how he feels about lunar independence," said Amos.

"I'm all for it." At that moment, I figured the less dealings with the moon the better. In fact, I was utterly in favor of the moon making a complete dash away from Earth's gravitational embrace.

Seth stepped forward. He had a thick beard and a missing front tooth. "We understand you've been sent here to spy on us," he said.

I looked around, trying to gauge the situation. "I wouldn't dream of spying on you, sir," I replied.

Seth gave me a hard look and held up the note Clarke had delivered to me. "Really?" He paused for effect, showing that no matter how rough one may look, there's always room for a hint of the dramatic. "You see, we have friends who watch out for our interests."

My heart skipped a beat. Not only because I'd been found out, but because the man could so casually hold a note that had taken a dip in the lunar sewers.

"Ah, yes. That was just a silly note from a friend."

Seth didn't seem convinced. "Really? Then why did you flush it?"

"It was an accident. Just dropped it in, really."

"We both know it was no accident," Maggie said, shaking her head. "You see, I had you made from the start, back on Earth, when I saw you take that note from that military fellow."

She had me there, so I decided to go on the offensive. Sure, they had me cornered in a cold room and tied up tighter than a drum, but I had come here to bargain. "Look, Maggie, boys, there's no reason to be upset. I never had any intention of spying on you or reporting you. I actually came here with a proposition."

"I have a proposition," Amos said, stepping forward. I couldn't help but notice he was carrying a big cleaver. "How about I gut you right here and grind you up for the meat?"

I was suddenly glad Maggie never got around to serving me that hamburger. I opened my mouth with the intention of putting up a good argument against that idea, but I found myself mostly gibbering. It's all rather indistinct, but I do believe I mentioned something regarding the Beckhams making disappointing hamburger meat.

Maggie spoke, silencing her menacing brood. "And what would a gentleman like you want with the likes of us?"

I cleared my throat. In my most earnest voice, I said, "I understand you removed several items from the collector Jasper White yesterday. I wish to obtain those items from you. I understand you sell them to a fence, or whomever, for a fraction of their true cost. I ask that you sell them to me at that reduced rate."

"And why should we?" Seth replied.

I attempted to shrug and found my bonds were too tight. "Well, you don't have to. However, it would save you a trip to your fence, and we would then be in league. You need not worry about me spying on you if we're in cahoots, and I'll even feed a little false information, nothing too harmful for king and country mind you, but I could say that I came to the cafe today, and I just met the beautiful owner and her charming sons, who gave no indication they were involved in anything nefarious. Sound like a deal?"

Seth looked to Maggie, who was considering my proposal. He shook his head to the negative. He started to turn towards Amos and his cleaver.

"I dare say," I uttered, a palpable strain shaping my vocal delivery. "I could even, perhaps, pay you a little bit more."

Seth emitted a guttural rumble, akin to a famished canine.

"A lot more money," I exclaimed. "I meant a lot more money."

Maggie placed her hand on Seth shoulder, restraining him with the gentle touch of maternal persuasion. "All right, Mr. Beckham. You have your deal. But I warn you, if you cross us, there's no place in this entire solar system where you can hide."

"I wouldn't dream of it, Maggie," I replied with a grin, hoping my abject terror would not show. "Let's go get that merchandise."

As we left the freezer, I couldn't help but feel a sense of relief. I had managed to get what I came for, and I had even made a new ally in the process. I couldn't wait to return to White and show him the recovered precious items.

§

That evening, while returning to Jasper White's mansion, I filled in Reggie, explaining how things had turned out. "I wish you could have been there to see me, Reggie. I was masterful in my negotiations. However, I was truly afraid for my life."

"I did take that into account when coming up with the plan, sir. The Campbell boys are well-known as ruffians and thieves, but they've never taken a human life, as far as the authorities know. While I expected them to be quite intimidating, I very much doubted you would come to any permanent harm."

"I really don't care to come to any temporary harm either, Reggie."

"I will remember that for future reference, sir."

As we pulled up to the house, I could see the scars of the attack from the Emerald Enforcers. Holes and cracks throughout the clear dome structure were patched with some kind of ugly brown material. Seeing the amount of damage, I couldn't help but feel a sense of trepidation.

"Reggie, do you think White will be angry with me, either for negotiating with the Emerald Enforcers or because he still thinks we were conspirators?"

"It's difficult to say, sir. However, in my experience these colonial magnates are quick to anger but regain their composure when their own interests are at stake. When I radioed news of our imminent arrival, his butler confirmed my supposition that he would have calmed himself since the attack."

As we entered the dome, I was greeted by White himself, who looked as if he had aged ten years in the past few days. "I must admit, Mr. Beckham, I was surprised to hear you were willing to show your face around here." His tone seemed more curious than accusatory, so I took that as a positive sign. "I hear you've brought me something."

"I am pleased to say, Mr. White, that at great risk to my own person, I have retrieved your items from the Emerald Enforcers. They're in our buggy, and your people may begin unloading them posthaste."

He froze for a moment, as if digesting new and unexpected information. "And what do you want in return, Mr. Beckham?"

"Only that you return to the negotiation table in good faith, giving me another chance to acquire the Gremlin."

Just then, the young woman who had greeted us the previous day hurried up to White. She carried one of the items we'd obtained from the Campbells, a large disk of clear plastic containing some moon dust stamped in an odd pattern. "Uncle Jasper, Uncle Jasper, it's here."

Jasper's eyes lit up and he took the disk from his niece. "Well, I'll be. I never thought I'd see this again. It's the center of my lunar collection, and worth more than all my automobiles combined." He held it up for us to see.

"Quite nice," I remarked, not seeing what was so great about it.

"This is one of the last remaining footsteps of Neil Armstrong, the first man to walk on the moon. It's a priceless historical relic, and the only one privately owned."

I nodded gravely, though I couldn't quite see why that old boot print was causing such a stir. I mean, even if it did belong to so-and-so's foot. Still, they did seem quite fond of this Armstrong fellow up here, what with all the this-and-that named after him.

"And the fact that I have it back, and in one piece, is a testament to your determination, Mr. Beckham," Jasper added.

I chuckled, trying to hide the relief in my voice. "Well, I couldn't have done it without the help of my associate, Reggie, of course."

Jasper seemed to deliberate for a moment, as though preparing to make a grand declaration. Finally, he made his announcement. "I tell you what, Mr. Beckham, there's no need for further negotiations. Why don't you have the old thing? Give me the address of your uncle's estate, and I'll have it shipped there."

"Oh, well then," I said in surprise. "Thank you very much, Mr. Jasper."

"Now, we were just about to sit down to dinner. Why don't you join us? I have an excellent chef and the finest wine cellar you'll find on the moon."

I gave him a half-bow. "It would be my honor, sir."

The dinner was magnificent, with course after course of delicious food and rich wine. Jasper regaled us with tales of his travels and adventures, and his niece, Lucinda, was a charming young woman, with sparkling eyes and a ready laugh. I found myself enamored with them both. As the night wore on, I found myself laughing and chatting with Jasper as if he were an old friend.

As we said our goodbyes, Jasper clapped me on the back. "You're a good man, Mr. Beckham. I look forward to doing business with you again."

I smiled. "As do I, Mr. White. As do I."

Reggie drove us back to our hotel so I could nap, as I'd consumed a large amount of wine over the course of the evening. I was just about to drowse off as something occurred to me, and I sat up straight. "I say! Reggie."

Reggie seemed unphased by my outburst. "What is it, sir?"

"What are we going to tell Colonel Clarke? We promised the Campbells protection. It seemed like a good idea when facing the meat grinder, but now I'm suddenly worried the old man will see it as a betrayal."

Reggie thought for a moment. "Did the Campbells at any time tell you they were part of the lunar independence movement?"

"Not as such—"

"Did you witness any evidence other than your temporary kidnapping which could have been an attempt to cover up criminal activities?"

"They did have a few odds and ends from Mr. White's collection in their possession."

"But you didn't see them personally take them?"

"I say, Reggie, isn't that splitting hairs just a bit?"

"Before I became your aunt's personal assistant, I worked in a junior capacity for Admiral George Sidney. At the time, he was running naval intelligence, and he would often complain to anyone who would listen that field operatives rarely provided definitive proof, and their language was often hedged to make clear determination impossible."

I thought about Reggie's words for a moment. "So, you're saying the more vague my report to the Colonel is…?"

"The more you will sound like the genuine clandestine agent."

"Oh. Well, thank you, Reggie."

He gave me an appreciative nod. "You are most welcome, sir."

After another moment's consideration, I asked, "Reggie, you wouldn't mind helping me draft that note?"

"In anticipation of your needs, sir, I have already drafted the note for you and forwarded it to Colonel Clarke."

"Oh. Very good then. Thank you, Reggie."

"You are most welcome, sir."

I let the gentle rocking of the buggy lull me back into sleep. The Gremlin was acquired, and I had a suitable report to share with Colonel Clarke which would not incur the wrath of the Emerald Enforcers. Soon, I would be back on Earth, but not before I had purchased a first-class ticket.

Shannon Ryan, a resident of Marion, Iowa, is an author specializing in urban fantasy and science fiction. Known for crafting narratives that seamlessly blend the peculiar with the humorous, his stories often feature characters as unconventional as satanic telemarketers and socially awkward vampires. Shannon balances his literary pursuits with an array of hobbies, including woodworking and computer programming. He also brings his keen eye to editorial projects. Away from the keyboard and workbench, Shannon enjoys unwinding with his feline companions.

Acknowledgements

I've been with Paradise ICON almost since the very beginning, and I've learned so much from every writer's group I've been part of, but especially this one. I appreciate greatly all the authors who contributed stories for this anthology – I'm very pleased with the results. Also, they are the ones who helped me grow into indie publishing.

We couldn't have this group without ICON, who hosts our group and often shares professional guests with us to learn from. Like our other anthologies, the proceeds will be donated back to ICON where we have made our home.

Thank you to Cath Schaff-Stump for leading us for so many years. Thanks to Cath Schaff-Stump, George Galuschak, Shannon Ryan, Stephanie Vance, and Athena Foster for assisting with the little things before I could get too stuck on anything. Many of my choices while learning to format this book echoed an anthology that Chris Cornell formatted, and while I wish he was here to tell me a few tricks, I appreciate having the example so I could remind myself if he figured it out, I could, too.

Thank you, Margot Foster, for the amazing cover design and for being fun to work with and even sometimes seeming to read my mind. Also much appreciation to Heather Tatarek of H2O Landscapes, an artist who also attends ICON, for the artwork that is the background of the cover.

Thank you, Emily Ender, for the random idea that became the story in this book, and, E.D. Martin, for support while I put the book together.

Mom, I wish I'd listened to you and done this earlier. I miss the support you always gave me, but I am buoyed by friends and writer-friends who also believe in me like you did. (Laurel Light, Dr. Jen Wojcik, Rebecca Greedy, and Reb Kreyling – I'm looking at you and grateful for you.) Honorable mention Keith Brandt – he knows why.

www.ingramcontent.com/pod-product-compliance
Lightning Source LLC
LaVergne TN
LVHW011839060526
838200LV00054B/4094